I WAS NEVER THE ONE

MUHAMMED ANSHID

Manda Publishers.com

Title: I WAS NEVER THE ONE

Author: MUHAMMED ANSHID

First Published by Manda Publishers in 2024

ISBN: 978-81-973481-3-6

Price in INR:249/-

Manda Publishers

www.mandapublishers.com

publish@mandapublishers.com

+91 9999190496

Cover Design: Harinandh S

Typography: Siddharth

Distributed by:

Amazon, Flipkart, Manda Publishers etc.

Printer:

Manipal Technologies Limited, Manipal

"I would like to express my sincere gratitude and love to everyone who stood by my side throughout this journey. Thank you for being there through thick and thin."

Contents

In my dreams I'm always with her

PART 1

ALL STARTS WITH A DREAM

JOHN KINGSTON UNDER THE SEA

LOVE HAS NO LOGIC THAT'S WHY IT'S CALLED MAGIC

TIME 6:27

John woke up after hearing a loud noise. It was an accident. John went to check out the cause of the noise but retreated upon seeing the scene. He witnessed a black and red Porsche car struck by a tree. He asked his neighbor about it, and he replied that it was the famous young businessman, "John Robert."

John Ethan Kingston was a well-known scientist who lived in England and had made a life for himself. He lost his parents when he was 17 years old and tragically lost his wife just a year into their marriage, when she was pregnant. This was why John hesitated to investigate the accident scene nearby; his fear of accidents stemmed from this personal tragedy. The incident had profoundly affected his life, leaving it in disarray. The fear of accidents and the loss of his loved ones continued to haunt him.

John was fed up with his life because nothing in it made him happy. He cried often, thinking about his family, and he almost gave up on life. He lived nearly 10 years without his wife, Isabel. John was a perfect gentleman who always brought happiness to people around him. Isabel was particularly joyful when she was with him; he constantly strived to make her the happiest, driven by his deep love for her. Her death profoundly changed him. He withdrew from others, developing a hatred towards everyone. John became a different person altogether, no longer the man who was deeply loved by someone. It was only after Isabel's death that John turned to drinking, eventually becoming an alcoholic.

One day, John was deeply saddened and upset because he had failed in one of his biggest research projects. He had invested so much hope and faith in it, but on that day, he broke down completely. He drank excessively and returned home, filled with hatred for his life, only to witness the death of his cat. This event left him feeling weary of life itself. The cat, named Isabel, was the sole reason he returned home; he spoke to it as if it were his late wife. John cried like a child, sitting on the floor and letting out loud sobs. He despised his life even more than before.

Two weeks passed, during which he remained secluded in his room, dwelling on his losses. His depression deepened. On that fateful day, he made the decision to visit his only uncle's house in the US, despite harboring resentment towards him. He chose to go because he held deep affection for Aunt Mary. When John's parents passed away, Aunt Mary had wanted to raise him, but his uncle had refused and sent him to an orphanage.

He decided to visit Aunt Mary one last time before ending everything. Already hating his life, this trip would be the final act in what he considered his most messed-up existence. John had always enjoyed traveling by ship, so he chose that as his mode of transport.

He donated everything he owned in Isabel's name. LIZANYAN 07 was the ship on which he traveled. One evening aboard, a small girl with curly hair approached him and asked to play. Before he could respond, her mother called her away. It was then that he learned her name was Sara. His eyes welled with tears, which he struggled to contain. Isabel had always dreamed of naming their child Sara.

"How beautiful it was when Isabel was with me," John thought.

Back when John was in the 7th grade, he had a crush on a girl named Rachel, who happened to be his neighbor and classmate. Despite their mutual feelings, Rachel's strict family instilled great fear in her. Overcoming his own fear, John confessed his love with the support of his friends.

Rachel knew he was genuine and decided to say yes to him and tell all her friends. She had that excitement, knowing she would have the guy whom she knew loved her so much. She returned home and smiled at all the letters he gave her. Yes, she loved him too. She couldn't stop smiling, but suddenly her mother caught her smiling at a letter, slapped her face, and asked about everything. Rachel had no choice but to tell her everything. Her mother scolded her severely. John was unaware of all these events.

The next day, a friend of Rachel told John everything that had happened and added that she had been ready to say yes, but now she couldn't because she was too afraid. The pain John suddenly felt was more than he could bear. His eyes started tearing up; he regretted writing that letter. Now he knew she wouldn't come back, yet he couldn't stop loving her. Seven years passed with the regret of that letter. He couldn't love anyone else after that; knowing she was once ready to accept him kept him hopeful.

Her smile, her eyes, her face—they kept him hanging on. He knew he could never love someone as much, not even half as much as he loved her. That day, he contemplated letting go of his feelings for her, but he knew he couldn't. She would never be his again; he knew his life would be ruined, and he chose to forget everything, even though he knew he never could. Destiny was against him when he was so close to her.

Everyone falls in love once. I, too, fell in love once, but I never anticipated how deeply it would affect me. I've tried countless times to erase her from my mind, but it's been impossible. I don't understand why it's so difficult for me. What was so special about her? Every time I see her, I feel the same as I did the first time. I loved her, fully aware she would never be mine. I loved her with all my heart, yet she didn't return my love. And now, finally, I'm ready to let go of everything. It took me seven years, but I will always keep a corner of her page folded in my book because it was one of my favorites. I've been with her so many times, even if only in my dreams. Sometimes, the best way to love is to let go. Now that I'm leaving her in this life, I hope that maybe in another life, she will be mine.

At the age of 17, John lost his parents in a car accident, leaving him orphaned. He spent a year in an orphanage before returning to live alone in his family home. John had always harbored dreams of becoming a great scientist like his father, which led him to enroll in college. Focused and studious, he immersed himself in his studies, devoid of any friends.

One day, at a science fair in college, a girl named Isabel approached him. It was a pivotal moment: John had showcased a machine capable of making objects disappear, though its destination remained a mystery. Isabel entrusted him with her blue-colored box, which promptly vanished upon activation. This encounter marked the beginning of their relationship.

Isabel sensed John's loneliness and reached out to him. They quickly became close friends, and her presence brought joy and companionship back into John's life. Loneliness faded away, replaced by a renewed sense of purpose and happiness. For the first time since his parents' death, John began to smile and feel alive again, thanks to Isabel's friendship and support.

The next year, Isabel proposed to John, which left him incredulous. John, known as an orphan with a simple, lonely, and somewhat introverted personality, couldn't believe that Isabel, the most admired girl in the entire college, had chosen him. Despite numerous admirers, Isabel's heart belonged to John, a fact that both amazed and deeply touched him. She affectionately called him "Ethan," a name he cherished hearing from her. Isabel cared for him with a tenderness akin to a mother's love, filling the void left by his parents' passing and transforming his bleak existence into a beautiful life.

Their love for each other grew deeper, and their relationship blossomed into perfection in every aspect. At the age of 25, John fulfilled his aspiration by assuming leadership of his father's laboratory, and he married Isabel, the love of his life.

However, their perfect life was disrupted one fateful day: February 7th, 2019—Isabel's birthday. John meticulously planned a surprise party for her that evening, pretending all day that he had forgotten her birthday to make the surprise even sweeter. Unfortunately, the day took a turn for the worse when there was an accident in his lab. A worker fell and was seriously injured, requiring hospitalization.

John became overwhelmed with tension, forgetting entirely about the planned birthday surprise due to the turmoil in his lab. Unaware of the chaos, Isabel repeatedly tried to reach him, but he was oblivious to her calls as his phone was out of reach. When finally handed his phone by a worker, he was confronted with a multitude of missed calls but chose to ignore them in his mounting frustration. Feeling like his head might explode, John, typically not one to stay out late, was pushed to his limits.

In a moment of pent-up emotion, he shouted at Isabel for the first time ever, causing her to recoil in fear, sensing that something serious had occurred.

Shortly thereafter, John received a call from the hospital informing him of Isabel's critical accident. The phone slipped from his grasp as he trembled uncontrollably, sweat beading on his forehead and his heart racing dangerously fast. Frantically repeating "she's alright" to himself, John tried to reassure himself during the frantic rush to the hospital.

Upon arrival, John dashed to the ICU, desperate for answers from the doctor. His pleas for Isabel's well-being fell into silence, and he was left to face the grim reality of the situation. Understanding the doctor's helplessness, John broke down in tears, continuing to implore for her life to be saved as he stood by her side in the ICU.

He held her tightly, weeping inconsolably. Reality hit hard when he realized she was lifeless, her body cold and unresponsive. Nurses offered their condolences, their apologies ringing hollow in the deafening silence that enveloped him. In that moment, the harsh truth sank in — she was gone.

Desperate, he clung to the hope that this was all a nightmare, pleading with himself to wake up and find her alive. His anguish poured out in tears, his sorrow palpable to those around him who struggled to comprehend his pain. His lips felt heavy, his voice silenced by the weight of grief that consumed him. Without her, he felt hollow, as if a vital part of himself had been torn away.

The realization that it was her birthday amplified his remorse. He blamed himself for everything — for not celebrating with her, for his outburst that led to her fateful drive. Regrets haunted him relentlessly, tormenting him with what-ifs and should-have-beens. He bore the unbearable weight of guilt, convinced he had caused her death.

Despite his overwhelming misery, he found himself unable to end his own life. Something deep within him, a faint glimmer of resilience or perhaps a force beyond his understanding, kept him clinging to existence, despite the darkness that threatened to consume him.

Now he hates himself every single day. He despises every day without her; without her, he feels like an empty soul. Nothing feels right to him anymore; she made him happy and complete. She illuminated his life. She saw him when he felt invisible. Now he is nothing but a soulless person waiting for his own death. She took his heart with her; she took the best part of him because she was the best part. Since then, he has felt like he's dying every day because pain is temporary, but regret is forever.

Suddenly, John heard an announcement from the ship's captain, Mr. Harvey, requesting everyone's presence in the ship's meeting hall for a meeting. The meeting was to discuss the ship's rules and regulations. Afterward, it was time for lunch, which John finished quietly.

He saw Sara playing with a doll in the corner, so he decided to go to her for a talk. For some time, he played with her, which eased his pain a bit. The second day, after noon, he felt so dizzy and tired that he decided to take a nap. Suddenly, he woke up after hearing a warning alarm. He ran out for checking about what is going on. There is a storm coming on the way, so the ship changes direction. The captain announces, “There is nothing to worry; we are changing our way; we are safe now,” reassured Captain Harvey over the ship's announcement system. John returned to his room and retrieved a photo from his pocket—it was a picture of Isabel. He whispered, "See you soon, my love."

Later that night, the ship's alarm sounded again as a storm with lightning struck. The ship began to sink, and panic ensued among the passengers. Everyone scrambled to escape in small boats, but John remained in his room.

He held Isabel's photo once more, kissing it with tears streaming down his face. Tears of relief, knowing he would soon reunite with his love.

Amidst the chaos, he heard a child crying. It was little Sara, stuck in her room. John kicked at the door in vain before spotting a hammer nearby. With a swift strike, he broke open the door and rescued Sara. He scooped her up and ran, the child crying in his arms. John frantically searched for Sara's parents, but they were nowhere to be found. Every boat had already departed, leaving them stranded.

As the ship descended into a massive whirlpool, John held Sara tightly, refusing to let go as they plunged into the depths together.

After a few minutes, John opened his eyes to find himself in a cave that shimmered with a dark blue hue, giving off an otherworldly glow. It wasn't like any ocean cave he had seen before; it felt surreal and mysterious. Thoughts of the Bermuda Triangle crossed his mind, wondering if this place had somehow transported him to a new world.

John recalled tales of the Bermuda Triangle where objects and people mysteriously vanished, sometimes reappearing in distant places or alternate realities. He pondered whether he had been transported to another universe or perhaps an underwater realm. The thought of being saved from certain death by some unknown force haunted him, leaving him feeling cursed to endure a life of perpetual darkness and misery.

His attention snapped back to the cave's contents, where he found all the items that had vanished when he experimented with his machine back in college, including Isabel's precious blue box. He clutched it tightly, feeling a surge of mixed emotions.

Suddenly, he remembered Sara. He called out for her, realizing she had been in his arms during the chaos but was now missing. His shouts echoed in the cavernous space, but there was no response. A beam of light caught his eye, emanating from a side of the cave. Instinctively, he followed it, hoping for an exit.

As he walked, the ground beneath him suddenly gave way, and he felt himself falling. Strangely, despite the sensation of falling, it felt more like descending gently. Eventually, he landed on solid ground and sprung to his feet. He couldn't believe what he saw.

Before him was a breathtaking sight—a majestic waterfall cascading down into a pool of crystal-clear water. The surroundings were surreal, with trees adorned with vibrant violet leaves and exotic fruits. Enchanting butterflies fluttered around, adding to the dreamlike atmosphere.

John stood there, bewildered and amazed. It felt like he had entered another realm altogether, a place that defied all logic and reason. For a moment, he wondered if he had passed into the afterlife, a paradise beyond the hardships of his earthly existence.

Everything was different there. The trees were very large with violet-colored leaves, and all of them bore fruits in beautiful shapes and colors. It felt like a model made of clay. Then he saw large birds, adorned with stars on their heads. The place was incredibly beautiful. Every tree was covered with butterflies, as if the butterflies were feasting on the trees. Then he encountered a massive waterfall. Feeling thirsty, he ran towards it and drank its water. The water tasted like pure wine. He enjoyed it so much that he drank a lot and eventually drifted off to sleep.

After some time, he woke up. He found himself in a jail cell, his legs bound with chains. He shouted, "Hellooooo... is anyone thereeee..." but received no reply. Eventually, a tall man appeared, whose appearance was strikingly different from ordinary people. His voice was loud, and he bore a scar on his face. He was a black man with long hair.

That man introduced himself to John; he said his name was Ashkan Fardobe. He was from a place called Monaskia.

Ashkan decided to help him get out of the cave without anyone noticing. Ashkan took a stone and broke the lock. They both ran before the army arrived, and in a flash, they reached a bustling town without any vehicles. The sights amazed John. The people there bore a striking resemblance to each other; while not identical, there were many similarities in their features and symmetry.

They were all black, tall, with long hair braided on both sides. Everyone had a beard, which appeared unkempt. Each person bore the same scar on their face, similar to Ashkan's. However, what intrigued John the most was that they were all men; not a single woman was among them. Suddenly, Ashkan covered John with a heavy jute cloth and stealthily escorted him to Ashkan's house without anyone noticing. Through the tiny holes in the jute, John caught glimpses of their surroundings. As they walked, he noticed houses that were all shaped like caves.

In a few minutes, they arrived home, and Ashkan helped John onto a stone bed. John was so exhausted that he fell asleep immediately. After a while, John woke up to the smell of something cooking. He tried to get up but found himself too weak to move. Murmuring to himself, he asked, "Where am I? Am I dead? Is this hell? Why does everything look so similar here? Why are there no women?" Ashkan heard John's questions and smiled faintly before handing him a cup of something to drink. Sitting beside John, Ashkan began, "This is not your world. Let me tell you about this world..."

Our world is completely different from yours. You could call it Earth 2. There are only three countries here: Lotrania, Woflia, and Giacia. We are currently in Lotrania, specifically in a place called Monaskia. The people here live tribally, and there are no women. Marriages occur between men, and they have children through that. The language spoken in this country is called Loturk. I believe I'm the only one here who understands your language.

This country has places like Monaskia, ElKosia, Lesokia, and Anmbria. Lesokia is inhabited solely by women; there are no men. In ElKosia, elves reside; the males are short, and the females are tall. Among these, Anmbria stands out as a unique place where only animals live. No humans are allowed to enter, and they possess the ability to communicate among themselves. They have their own set of rules and a king who changes annually to govern them.

Woflia and Giacia are highly perilous countries; no one has ever returned from there. I cannot confirm if these stories are real or fabricated because I have never been there myself. It is said that Woflia is inhabited by malevolent witches who are exceedingly cruel and reportedly sacrifice humans to fulfill their desires. In Giacia, giants of immense stature are said to reside, towering as tall as mountains.

John became apprehensive and questioned Ashkan about his knowledge of English and how he became acquainted with details about John's world.

Ashkan replied, "I lived in your world for 11 months. Once, I accidentally fell into a wormhole just like you came here, and it transported me to your world. A man there helped me; he taught me your language and shared everything about your people and country."John, then how did you come back?

Ashkan explained further, "The person who helped me was a great scientist named Joseph Kingston. His research focused on other universes, and he used his technologies to open a portal for me. That's how I returned here. He referred to this world as Earth 2. You resemble him, which is why I decided to help you. I'll always remember that person, and I truly hope he's still happy and healthy."

A current passed through John's body, causing him to shiver with tears filling his eyes. He said, "No, he died in a car accident."

Ashkan: heh! Do you know him?

John: My name is John Ethan Kingston, son of Joseph Kingston; he's my father.

Ashkan hugged John. Ashkan couldn't believe his eyes.

Ashkan said, "Maybe this is something the world has planned to do to help his son for what that great man has done to help me. This is destiny; I will help you no matter what."

John: How can you help me?

Ashkan replied, "I don't exactly know how, but we have a legend here that says there is a temple of King Poseedios where there are a lot of treasures and a statue. If you hold the hand of the statue and make a wish from your heart, that wish will happen." John, filled with curiosity and excitement, asked if this legend was true. Ashkan nodded affirmatively and suggested that to learn more about it, they should seek guidance from someone. John then asked who that person was.

Ashkan: We should go to Lesokia to visit a woman who is 5037 years old.

John: what! People live 5037 years here.

Ashkan proudly said, "Yes, and I'm 1199 years old, and I'm considered young here. By the way, tomorrow is my birthday."

John: In advance, Happy Birthday, bro.

Ashkan said, "Thank you. We should visit her now, and she will guide us to the temple. There, you can find a way back to your home."

John: Ashkan That's not what I want.

Ashkan: Wait, what!? You don't want to return?

John responded, "There is nothing left for me here; I lost my world so long ago that I want to bring it back. I want to bring Isabel back to life; that's my wish. She's my world, my home; she's everything I have ever wished for, the only one I had, and I killed her." John explained all that had transpired in his life to Ashkan. Ashkan's eyes filled with pain upon hearing the story. He said, "I don't know if we could bring someone back to life, but until my last breath, I swear I will help you reach the temple."

They embarked on their journey towards the women. It was a long way, and along the path, John noticed many beautiful and surreal sights. He had a million questions swirling in his mind, but he kept

them to himself. His thoughts were consumed by Isabel and the hope of bringing her back. After a lengthy walk, they arrived at Lesokia.

John observed that all the people there were indeed women, just as Ashkan had mentioned earlier. They were tall and fair-skinned, with the same scar as the Monaskians. In Lesokia, the scar was on the right side of their faces, while in Monaskia, it was on the left. When John inquired about this, he learned that the scar on Monaskians and Lesokians originated from a curse inflicted by witches who resided in Magicia, a region within Woflia. These witches were described as frightening and malevolent, harboring deep animosity towards Monaskians and Lesokians. It was their curse that marked everyone in Monaskia and Lesokia with the scar on their faces.

They approached a woman and inquired about the old lady they were supposed to meet. Without hesitation, she replied, "She's a real eccentric; nobody visits her. Her name is AsheeraWaltain." She pointed towards Asheera's house and promptly departed.

They approached her house, which was nestled within a tree. People in this community lived inside large trees, crafting their homes within them. Ashkan called out Asheera's name. She made strange sounds, murmured to herself, and eventually emerged from her dwelling. John was deeply surprised by her appearance. Despite being 5037 years old, she appeared to be only 20-25 years old. Her demeanor exuded confidence, and John observed that all the women in Lesokia appeared youthful and beautiful, leading him to believe that they did not age.

Asheera invited them inside, and Ashkan conversed with her in the Loturk language. After a brief discussion, Asheera turned to John and asked for his name in English. John was surprised and asked, "How do you know English?" Asheera replied, "Child, I've lived for 5037 years. What can I not know?" After a moment of silence, she continued, "You are here to learn about that temple, aren't you? I cannot assist you with that. You may leave now." John pleaded with her, "Please, we need your help."

Asheera replied, "People believe the temple is merely a made-up story because those who went in search of the treasure never returned. But I know it's because of their greed; they may have been punished. If you seek the treasure, I will say no more."

John replied firmly, "No, we're not going for the treasure. We're going to see the statue that grants wishes. I want my wife back; I'm doing this for my love."

Asheera nodded and said warmly, "That's good; you are doing this for love. It's pleasant to hear that the things people do for their love are unbelievable. I will share whatever I know with you."

John: Tell us the way to the temple, then.

Asheera: Before that, you should know about the king Poseedios and his history.

He was the king of Lotrania 10,000 years ago. He possessed great abilities and magical powers, known only to his trustworthy minister. Renowned for his benevolence, he was also the wealthiest monarch in the realm. The king had four brothers, each with their own ambitions. One fateful day, he summoned them all for a crucial meeting, declaring his intent to donate his vast wealth to the poor and needy upon his demise. This proclamation greatly displeased his greedy and short-sighted brothers, who sought to eliminate the king before he could announce his decision to the entire kingdom.

The foolish brothers approached the king's minister to carry out their plan. Leading them to believe he would cooperate, the minister instead revealed their intentions to the king. Upon hearing this, the king didn't react with anger toward his brothers; rather, he felt sorrow for them, knowing they would never inherit his wealth.

Utilizing his magical abilities, the king concealed all his riches within the temple, securing them with a complex puzzle. Only those who were both courageous and exceptionally intelligent could hope to solve the puzzle and claim the treasure.

After that, the king confronted his brothers knowing they had poisoned his food, and he consumed it willingly. King Poseedios's body was laid to rest in a pyramid. Shortly after the king's passing, his loyal minister also passed away. As his trusted advisor, the minister was buried alongside the king in the same pyramid. Following these events, the four greedy brothers returned to the palace to claim the king's wealth. They were astonished upon opening the treasure vault; there wasn't a single gold coin to be found. However, one of them noticed a letter left behind.

The letter contained three symbols: a pyramid with a sword on it, a temple, and a key tree. The four foolish brothers couldn't decipher the meaning of these signs. They searched everywhere for the treasure, but their efforts were in vain.

So many years passed, and many people went searching for the treasure. Those who discovered that King Poseedios had hidden all the treasure inside a temple ventured out, but they never returned.

After explaining the story, Asheera asked if they were sure they wanted to go. Ashkan firmly replied, "Yes, we are doing it at any cost."

John then asked, “You told us about the treasure but not about the statue that grants wishes."

Asheera responded, "I can't assure you about the statue. It was mentioned by the minister to his wife a few days before his death. Even I don't know if that's true. That minister was from Monaskia; he was the first and only one to marry a woman from Lesokia, and because of that, they didn't have any children."

John: If there is a single ray of hope, I'm going to risk it with my life; no matter what's going to happen, I will face it.

Asheera: "Fine, then I will tell you the way to it. First, you need to cross ElKosia to find the pyramid where King Poseedios was buried. Inside the king's tomb, you will find a sword. Be very careful when taking the sword. There are five pyramids, and if you enter any of the other four, you won't return. After retrieving the sword from the correct pyramid, your next task is to find a magical tree.

No one knows its exact location, but it becomes visible only on a full moon night, glowing brightly. To see the tree, you must touch the sword; otherwise, it will remain invisible to you."

"The tree will be visible once a month during the full moon. This tree bears a fruit that contains the key to the temple. Obtaining it won't be easy; there will be formidable protections around the tree that you must overcome. After securing the key, your final task is to locate the temple. These are the only pieces of information I have," Asheera explained.

"Out of everyone I have met so far, I believe you will find it because love never fails to amaze. Love can do magic," Asheera said with a warm smile.

I have two clues to find the correct pyramid.

Everything looks exactly the same, but the real one is different.

Only those who have light in their hearts can find it.

"These are the two clues that the minister told his wife; you will find more clues when you find the sword," Asheera continued.

She wished them luck. John and Ashkan started their journey to fight for love. They gathered everything they needed and set off. After a long walk, they felt tired and sat under a tree to take a nap.

Ashkan opened his eyes to find that they had been tied up by ropes, surrounded by elves. Next to them was a big bowl of water being boiled, the elves' method for dealing with enemies. All the elves had large ears and sharp noses, each wearing a necklace adorned with an ear. John was wonderstruck when he woke up to witness this scene.

Ashkan tried to talk to them, but they didn't even give him an ear to listen. When Ashkan began to speak, they beat him with a stick and laughed loudly.

Among them, an elf who appeared elderly instructed the others to kill the giants before they got out of control, mistaking John and Ashkan for giants. Ashkan, frustrated, shouted loudly, "We are not giants! We are not here to harm you; we are trying to find the temple of King Poseedios." Upon hearing this, the elves burst into hearty laughter. However, their king approached after overhearing the commotion and remarked, "The magic temple isn't real; it's all a made-up story. No one has ever found the temple." Ashkan translated the conversation for John.

John: "I will... I will find the temple. Please, leave us be. If you let us go now, I promise to bring all the gold to you."

Elf King: Why should I trust a giant?

John: I am not going for the treasure; I am going to make a wish of mine to get my love back.

Saying this, his eyes were flooded with tears. The king noticed the truth of John's love and his tears.

Elf King: So, you are here for love, right? Fair enough, we will set you free, but tonight you will stay here, and we will provide the best party you have ever had in your life.

By hearing this, all the other elves shouted, "Kill the giants!" The king intervened, asserting, "I am the king. I order that they be treated as our guests. Treat them well." As night fell, the elves provided them with a hut to rest. Sitting there, John's thoughts were consumed by memories of her. Gradually, the sounds of celebration grew louder, and they noticed the elves dancing with drinks in hand. They invited Ashkan and John to join, offering them drinks. John stood awkwardly amidst the festivities. He attempted to dance but found himself unable to.

The king observed John's discomfort and invited them to his quarters. After some initial conversation, the king turned to John and asked, "You risk your life for your wife, so she must be a remarkable woman. What happened to her?" John felt a lump in his throat, the pain evident in his expression. He recounted the story, concluding with a choked voice, "I killed her," tears streaming down his face despite his efforts to hold them back.

Hearing this, the king embraced John warmly, saying, "I can feel your pain. I lost my wife too, the queen of the elves. Just like you, I still can't forget her. She was my everything; she loved everyone equally in my country, and for that, she sacrificed herself."

"She was the daughter of the king of ElKosia; nobody ever saw her face except her father and mother because she always covered it. Her name was El Nina. People speculated about her appearance—some said she was ugly, hence the veil, while others claimed she was the most beautiful girl in the world. She visited the town weekly, known for her kindness and generosity toward the poor. El Nina enjoyed games and often engaged with the townsfolk, always accompanied by numerous security guards for protection."

"I was working in a clothing shop one day when she visited and asked me to gather all the beautiful dresses in my store. Initially, I assumed they were for her, but she bought them for the needy. She requested that I keep this act of kindness confidential. Curious, I asked her why she always covered her face—was it because she was exceptionally beautiful or considered unattractive? She left without a response. Later, as she distributed the dresses, she discovered they were the same ones she had purchased from my shop. Intrigued, she inquired about their origin and learned that I had provided the dresses. She was impressed by my gesture."

The next day, she came again. She asked me what my name was. I told her I'm El Rom.

El Nina: Mr. El Rom, what do you think about me? Look into my eyes and say,.

El Rom: I can see the moon in your eyes.

I fell for her when I looked into her eyes.

"She laughed and departed. The following day, near closing time, El Nina returned without any security guards, dressed plainly to avoid attention. She asked me to show her around, and this became a regular occurrence. I introduced her to the finest spots in ElKosia, and we both relished our time together. Gradually, we fell in love."

"One day, she said she had a surprise for me and took me to an empty cave. She asked me to close my eyes. Counting slowly, 'One, two, three,' she instructed. When I opened my eyes, I was overwhelmed and lost consciousness. She had revealed her face to me—it was the most beautiful sight I had ever beheld in my life. I couldn't believe it. How could someone be so stunning? Her beauty was like a ray of sunshine, capable of brightening any place."

"Her beautiful smile never fails to melt my heart. Her kindness, compassion, and unwavering support have touched my soul deeply. When we're together, the world fades away, and all that matters is the love we share. I'm grateful for how she made me feel seen, heard, and loved just as I am. She turned my life into a beautiful love story."

"This continued every day; every day I loved her a bit more, every day I saw love in her eyes, and every day I found more love."

We have a group of elves here called Nyelves who hate the king. One day they saw El Nina with me; they made a plan and kidnapped her the next day. I didn't know about this; I waited for her at our place for so long. The next day, a soldier from the palace came to the town and announced, "Princess El Nina has been missing since yesterday; if anyone sees her, come to the palace now; the person who finds her will be treated with great rewards.".

"I was scared; I didn't know what had happened to her. But I knew who did this. Only Nyelves dare to do this to a princess. I knew their whereabouts; they always lived inside caves, and they had a different dressing style. They were my daily customers; we made their dresses, so I dressed like them and started to search for her. I searched for her in every cave where they lived. Finally, I found her in one, but I couldn't free her because there were so many Nyelves there at that time."

I didn't see any way to help her; that's when I got this idea. I lifted her face cover, and everyone who saw her face fell unconscious because of her beauty. We both escaped from there.

The King appreciated me for helping her and offered me big rewards, but I told him I didn't want any rewards. I love El Nina, and we both love each other. Please give her to me. El Nina agreed too, and the king arranged our marriage. After some years, the king died, and I became the new king of ElKosia. We lived peacefully. One day, I received the good news that El Nina was pregnant, which sparked the biggest party in ElKosia. Everyone enjoyed it, but all the men and guards became drunk and lost consciousness.

The next day, many young ladies went missing. At that time, I received a letter from a black raven. The letter was from a wicked witch from Magicia who sacrifices human lives. The letter demanded that I bring 20 young, beautiful ladies to them before sunset, or they would burn ElKosia. I understood their intentions. They sacrificed young, beautiful ladies for their needs because they were so ugly and horrible. They believed that sacrificing beautiful ladies would make them beautiful.

I told El Nina about this, and she became very sad. She told me we had to do something; we couldn't let those poor people die. I told her there was nothing we could do. They are so powerful, and we can't do anything. The next day, she went to them alone, without any guards. She asked the witches to release all of them and take her instead. Every witch laughed at her. She then removed her face cover, and everyone fell silent. The witches started jumping for joy. They got what they needed.

El Nina asked them to spend one last night with me. They agreed to that. Everyone thought El Nina saved the ladies, and we had a big victory party that day. She didn't let me join in on it. She slept on my lap all night. The next day, a young lady who had gone missing came to me and told me about their agreement. I couldn't believe it. I searched for her everywhere but couldn't find her anywhere. She sacrificed herself for everyone; she was pregnant, but she only cared about the people.

I still miss her every single day, but I will always cherish the memories of her. She was an amazing person and a beautiful soul, full of kindness, compassion, and a zest for life. I remember her contagious laughter and the way she brought joy everywhere she went. It's been seven years since then, and I hope her soul rests in peace.

They ended her life.

Not my love

They killed her.

Not my feelings

They took her away.

Not her memories

They separated our bodies.

Not our souls

El Rom added, "I believe you will find your love; I know that's the only way to heal your heart. Once a heart is hurt by love, only love can heal it."

El Rom gave them something they could use for their journey, and they resumed their travels. They reached a forest where they saw five pyramids, all identical. John had never imagined seeing pyramids in a forest before.

All the pyramids looked identical; they didn't know which one was real or how to find it. John pondered Asheera's two clues for a while. Then, John instructed Ashkan to cut down the trees that faced the sun.

That day, both of them cut down the trees. The next morning, as the sun rose, the pyramids were bathed in sunlight, and only one cast a shadow. Ashkan leaped for joy and asked, "How did you know that?" John replied, "Do you remember the two clues Asheera gave us? 'Everything looks exactly the same, but the real one is different; only the one who has light in their heart can find it.' I just pondered on it."

They both knew there might be something dangerous inside the pyramid as they attempted to enter. It was so dark that they couldn't see beyond their noses. Ashkan lit a torch. They discovered a plain wall with no visible door. John felt hopeless, but Ashkan noticed a differently colored stone and touched it hastily. Suddenly, the walls collapsed silently, allowing them entry.

Inside, they found King Poseedios's tomb. Ashkan moved to open it eagerly, but John stopped him, recalling Asheera's words. "You should stand back from the tomb; it might be dangerous. Let me open the door, and on the count of three, we'll run." Ashkan nodded, and John slowly opened the tomb door. As Ashkan counted "1... 2... 3...," they both dashed away, but nothing happened. They cautiously returned to find the tomb empty—no sword, no sign of the king's body.

John felt disheartened and remarked, "Yes, they were right. It was all just a made-up story."

They both had lost hope and were ready to leave when Ashkan noticed another tomb near the king's tomb—it was the minister's tomb. He opened it, called John over, and they found the sword inside. Ashkan noticed the name on the tomb: TysomerWaltain. They were both surprised. John exclaimed, "That means AsheeraWaltain is the wife of the minister, and she isn't 5037 years old; she is more than 10,000 years old."

They pulled out the sword and suddenly heard a noise; lava began to flow from all directions inside the pyramid. They realized the pyramid was about to collapse. They sprinted out of the pyramid just in time and managed to escape.

Once outside, they saw that the other four pyramids had vanished, and the real pyramid they had been inside was sinking into the ground. In a matter of moments, the entire place had vanished.

Now armed with the sword, they noticed something carved into it. To decipher its meaning, they decided to return to the old lady, Asheera. On their way back, they encountered El Rom and shared the news of their discovery. He was overjoyed to hear it.

They arrived in Lesokia and discovered that no one there knew anyone named AsheeraWaltain. John and Ashkan were astonished; they had met her just weeks before, but now she was referred to as "Crack Head" by the locals, and she seemed to have vanished from memory. They speculated that perhaps the minister had assigned her the task of aiding those seeking the temple. Determined, they approached everyone in the village to see if anyone could decipher the inscription on the sword. Eventually, a woman agreed to read it. She revealed that it contained the next clue to finding the magic tree.

Only the one with a colorful heart can find it.

This was the clue written on the sword.

Ashkan: We only know about the full moon. Where will we go to search for the tree?

John: I know how to.

Ashkan: how?

John: Which is the largest mountain here?

Ashkan: It's Mount Mozrak. We can see the whole of Earth 2 from there, but it's too risky to climb there.

John: fine. That's where we are going to go next. We will find the tree from there.

Ashkan was happy to hear that idea, and they started their journey to find the magic tree.

John asked how many days were left until the full moon, and Ashkan replied, "20 to 25 days." John realized they needed to reach their destination quickly.

They embarked on their journey to Mount Mozrak. After traveling a great distance, they finally reached the mountain and discovered a solitary house there.

They approached the house to see if anyone was inside, and discovered a woman living there alone. They spoke with her, and she graciously offered them food and shelter for the night. Curious about their quest, she questioned Ashkan about their search for the temple, warning them of its dangers. Ashkan replied, "He is searching for his love." The woman smiled knowingly, recognizing the power of love.

She cautioned them, "You should be careful when climbing Mozrak. 'Mozrak' means 'death' in the Loturk language, and true to its name, it is extremely dangerous. I lost my wife and child on its summit."

There are many dangerous animals on the mountain, and we can't defend ourselves if they attack us. At the summit, there is a fruit that my daughter loves dearly. One day, my daughter Yelihra insisted on having that fruit. She longed for it intensely, and it was nearly evening. I warned them, "Don't go now; evening is approaching." But she was adamant, so we packed our bags and began our ascent.

On our way, we heard eerie noises in the distance. As the sound drew closer, we hurried to find a hiding place.

We spotted a large animal searching for us; fortunately, it didn't notice us at that moment. The creature was enormous, walking on two legs like a human. Sometime later, we cautiously emerged from hiding. I insisted we should retreat, as it was too perilous to stay. We agreed to leave and return another time.

On our way back, the same creature found us again, and we fled in terror. During our escape, Yelihra dropped her bag and went back to retrieve it. Tragically, the creature caught her then and devoured her right before our eyes.

Seeing this, my wife rushed towards the creature and met the same fate as our daughter. The creature then turned towards me, but suddenly a small insect called Mozeetus appeared and bit it, causing it to collapse unconscious. I was stunned and unsure of what to do next. Unable to comprehend the situation, I wished desperately that it was all just a dream and fled back home.

I returned to the site in the morning and found only Yelihra's bag. There were large footprints left by the creature. Ashkan asked how big the footprints were. The woman replied that they were as large as a Korpes. Saying this, the woman began to cry. Ashkan hugged her gently, offering comfort.

Ashkan asked her how she managed to live alone like this. She replied, "With their memories. Memories are forever; everyone leaves, but memories stay. You don't need anyone if you have memories, and you don't need a good friend if you have good memories. Memories endure even after death. They are special, even if they are painful. There's nothing in the world that's permanent except memories. Forever is reserved only for memories, not for people. I live with their memories, but I'm weary of living alone."

Ashkan liked her a bit.

Ashkan said, "If you're tired of living alone, come with me. I'll take care of you. It doesn't matter if you're a woman; you can stay with me. I'm also living alone like you." Hearing this, she hugged him and replied, "I don't know if I can leave from here; their memories stay here. But I'd love to come with you. I'm tired of living alone."

Ashkan declared, "I will come back for you after we find the temple, I promise. I'll give you a good life, make you the happiest, and love you until I die. That's my promise."

She gave him a small smile of acceptance and nodded her head. Both of them became happy.

Seeing all this, John was overjoyed for his brother Ashkan. He hugged him tightly, thrilled that Ashkan had found his love.

John: Now I understand that you always liked women, right? That's why you are not yet married and living alone.

Ashkan: Yeah, I'm a big fan of Minister TysomerWaltain. Ha-ha.

Both of them laughed together. The next morning, they prepared themselves to climb Mount Mozrak. Setting off on their journey, the woman had given them a shortcut to reach the summit. They ascended for a long while and eventually reached a small waterfall, where they replenished their water supply. With plenty of time left due to the shortcut, they decided to take a break. They drank from the waterfall and rested, taking a nap under a nearby tree.

John woke up to realize it was night time and the full moon was approaching soon. They realized they had been asleep for almost 10 days. John was bewildered by how this could have happened. Ashkan then noticed small bite marks on them. They had been bitten by a small insect called Mozeetus. Ashkan explained that it was a tiny, poisonous insect similar to a mosquito. Its venom had caused them to sleep for days. He speculated that even the large creature they encountered earlier might have avoided them due to the insect's poison.

John began to run, shouting, "We have no time left; we must reach the top of the mountain!" They pressed on without rest to reach their destination. Upon arrival, they quickly set up a tent and lit a fire. With only one day remaining until the full moon, they sharpened their focus.

When night fell and the moon reached its full phase, they both touched the sword. Suddenly, the moon's color shifted to blue, and its light illuminated the magic tree.

Ashkan shouted, "John, the magic tree!" John and Ashkan saw the tree glowing in the dark. Ashkan urged, "We have to move fast; we need to get there before the next full moon." John paused and said, "Wait, I need to see how long it will keep shining." They watched as the light gradually began to fade. John estimated the distance to the tree and concluded, "We have almost 30 minutes to get the fruit from the tree. We need to move quickly to reach it in time."

They spent the night in the tent, knowing they had only 30 more days to reach the magic tree. The next morning, they began their journey in the direction of the tree. Realizing they wouldn't reach it in time by walking, they decided to steal horses, as they had no money to buy them. Ashkan led John to a farm, but instead of horses, they found strange animals with three legs and two horns on their heads. John asked where the horses were. Ashkan smiled and replied, "These are our horses here; we call them Korpes."

That night, ensuring no one was around, they stole two of the strange creatures known as "Korpes" and began their journey on the LotranianKorpes. To John's surprise, the Korpes were faster than he had anticipated. After extensive riding, they finally reached a new location.

It was really dark, and slowly rain started pouring. Ashkan looked afraid. John asked the reason.

Ashkan: I never thought this place was this scary. I heard about it before and thought it was just a story, but no. This is the place Elf King El Rom mentioned; this is Magicia, in Woflia. The cruelest witches live here and sacrifice humans for their needs. We need to find another way. This seems like a suicide mission.

John: No, we don't have enough time, and we don't know how to find another way. We have to take this risk. If you are scared, you can leave. I don't fear death; my heart has been dead all these years. Now I see a glimpse of hope to get my life and my love back, and I am willing to risk anything for it. But I don't insist you follow my reckless path.

Ashkan: If you are going, then I am too, no matter what.

They dismounted from the Korpes and sent them away. As they walked forward, they saw a massive, eerie mansion. Though terrified, they pressed on. Suddenly, a hand touched Ashkan, causing him to scream loudly. John turned to see a little girl standing there. They asked her who she was and why she was there. She replied, "Don't be scared. I will not harm you. I'm here to help you. You should come with me." With no other options and their lives already in danger, they decided to follow her.

They reached a large tree where the girl stopped and took a red stone out of her large black hood. She threw it at the tree, and slowly, the roots moved aside, creating a path inside. She welcomed them in, and once they entered, the roots closed the way behind them.

John, still wary, asked, "Who are you? Why are you helping us? Is this a trap? If you want to kill someone, kill me. Let him go, please."

The girl removed her hood. John cried upon seeing her face. He hugged her. Ashkan was really amazed.

Ashkan: What's going on here? Who is she?

John: Her name is Sara; she was with me when the ship wrecked. What happened to you? How did you end up here? Wait, are you really my Sara? Because she was very small. But you are 4-5 years older.

Sara: Yes, I am Sara. I have been here for almost 7 years.

John: what? No way; we were both on the same ship, and I have been here for only 3 months. Then how did that happen?

Sara: "I don't really know. The last thing I remember was you holding me tightly.

And I had an unforgettable dream at that time; in that dream, I was in another place, like a haunted house. I was so scared. I was trapped in that house for two days. Suddenly, a boy and a girl came to help me. They got me out of there. That place was so different and scary. There we had no hunger or thirst, no mornings or nights; every day was the same. They told me it's a dream world, and we are living in it. They comforted me, and at that time I noticed I grew older. I don't know how that happened. I don't understand anything there.

I forgot the name of the girl, but the boy's name was John, and he looked exactly like you, but younger. They were not on our ship; they said they were trapped there while sleeping. All of us made a tent and stayed there. Then, a friend of theirs who had gone missing returned. He told us he found a way to escape from there.

He showed us a red light flashing in the sky. He told us there were big buildings there; perhaps there would be people who could help us escape. We set out towards it. Suddenly, a shadow emerged from nowhere and enveloped us. We could see nothing but the flashing light. Soon after, all of us fell unconscious.

Sara paused for a while, her eyes starting to water slightly. John came near and held her close, encouraging her to continue.

"And when I opened my eyes, I was lying here on the ground. It was just a dream," she said, her voice trembling. "I woke up and cried loudly. Nobody heard me until a witch came to me and took me with her. I'm alive because of Queen El Nina. The witches took her from ElKosia to sacrifice her life for their needs. At the same time they took me, they were so happy, but El Nina begged them for me, and because of her, I'm still alive. They tortured me. They made me a witch. I'm tired of this life. I hate being here."

Sara started crying.

John; I'm so sorry, Sara. Come with us; we will get you out of here.

Sara replied firmly, "No, I can't leave Magicia. But I can help you get out of here. We don't have time, or else you will be dead."

John: I'm so sorry. I'm the one who brought you here; let's get out here together.

Sara: I can't escape Magicia; I can never leave here, and it's not your fault. Come, you should leave now.

They walked a long way and arrived at a large door adorned with intricate carvings. Sara stopped beside it and said, "I cannot come any further; you can go now." John felt torn about leaving her behind; the pain was unbearable. Sara handed him a vial of magic liquid, instructing him to use it if he encountered danger. The liquid had the power to alter the appearance of anything. Sara looked at John solemnly and said, "All of this happened because of your father; he was the first one to open the portal. Because of him, all of this happened."

After Sara left, John wanted to ask her many questions, but couldn't. He looked at Ashkan, who said, "She is right. Your father was a great scientist. His research was all about different parallel worlds. He created a machine and made a portal, but he couldn't control it, and I got trapped in it. He tried tirelessly to reopen the portal, which seemed impossible. Eventually, he managed to open it and rescue me. However, I don't think he was able to destroy it, and somehow the portal expanded to many places."

John replied, "No, it's not him; it's me. It's all because of me. I opened the portal. I used my father's technology to find Isabel, to create a new world, and it all ended in failure. My father successfully closed every portal he opened, but I reopened it. Because of me, Sara is here, and everything happened because of me."

Ashkan responded, "Don't blame yourself for everything. Maybe all these things happened for a reason; maybe it's for you to find Isabel."

John felt a bit relieved, and they left Magicia. With the full moon approaching, they hastened their journey. After measuring the distance, they set up a tent.

Ashkan noticed John thinking about something and asked what had happened and what he was thinking. John replied it's Sara; I couldn't forget her face. She is suffering because of me.

She's not smiling.

She never stopped smiling.

She's not talking.

She never stopped talking.

I took her light.

I am the reason somehow.

Now her face seems cold.

She won't smile anymore.

She talks no more.

I saw her living but lifeless in her eyes.

Ashkan: It's not your fault; like I said, everything happens for a reason.

John: No. I can't do this; we should go back to Magicia and help her.

Ashkan: How are we going to help her? They are too powerful.

John: We'll figure that out. That's what we always do, right?

Ashkan: It's almost full moon day; we should focus on this.

John: I know, but I will never be happy knowing Sara is suffering here because of me. I think we should help her first, and we can come back next month.

Ashkan agreed with him, and both of them went back.

They left some marks there to find that place again, and they went to Magicia. The moment they entered the Magicia, Sara felt that and went to them.

Sara, "Why did you come back? You shouldn't be here, please leave."

John: No, we are not leaving without you. Come with us. We will protect you with our lives.

Sara: I can't come. I'm not staying here because I'm afraid of death. I'm staying here for her; I'm staying here for El Nina.

Ashkan: what!! Isn't she dead? How is she still alive?

Sara: No. They brought her to sacrifice her life, but not now. They will kill her after 3 months.

John: Why?

Sara: They are waiting for the Red Moon Day; it only happens once every 100 years. In three months, the Red Moon Day will arrive, and they plan to sacrifice her life. They believe it will make them the most beautiful people in the world. That's why they've kept her here this long. And because of her, I'm staying here. They told me if I ever try to escape from Magicia, they will torture her every day, and I can't let that happen. That's why I can't come with you until she dies.

John and Ashkan exchanged a solemn look, realizing the gravity of the situation and the urgency to act before the fateful Red Moon Day arrived.

Ashkan: What happened to her child?

Sara: They killed the child the next day they caught El Nina because they were afraid she was losing her beauty.

John and Ashkan narrated the Elf King's story to Sara.

John: El Rom is a good man, and he is suffering from a lot of pain. I can see a dead man inside that small body.

Ashkan: We should help El Nina. We came for you, Sara, but we are going to get you both out of here.

John: Sara… Tell me about this place.

Sara: Ok. This country is called Woflia, and here there are three places: Magicia, Horeefia, and Glorfia. They all hate each other and are constantly fighting. Magicia is the cruelest of all three. Once, during a major conflict between them, the witches in Magicia cast a spell preventing any other Woflians from entering Magicia. If any magician leaves here, they will know about it. The one thing I understood was that they are all foolish; they know magic and witchcraft, but they are stupid.

John and Ashkan listened intently, absorbing the information about the complex dynamics of Woflia and the severe consequences of magic use within Magicia.

Ashkan: How do we find El Nina? Where is she?

Sara: She's in a prison made of rocks, and it is protected by large, cruel animals outside. Only witches can enter the prison.

John: Okay, I have to think.

After thinking for some time, John came up with an idea.

John: You know magic, right, Sara?

Sara: Yes, a little bit.

John: Fine. Can you make us look like witches?

Sara: Yes, I can, but it will only last one hour or less. You just look like them; you will not have any powers.

John: Okay, perfect. I have an idea. Are you ready, Mr. Fardobe?

Ashkan: Yes, sir...

Sara, with her powers, made them look like witches. The three of them went to the prison. Along the way, they saw many skeletons of people, creating a very eerie atmosphere. The distant sound of thunder and flashes of lightning startled them. Nevertheless, they pressed on and soon arrived near the prison, which appeared larger than they had anticipated. Just then, Sara approached it. Two large animals emerged from within; they resembled big dogs. Sara attempted to approach them, but they advanced towards the group. John drew his sword, and upon seeing it, both animals swiftly retreated. It was then that they realized the power held within that sword.

They entered the prison. Sara led them to El Nina's cell. Spotting her, they approached, but she was scared and backed away. Speaking softly, they reassured her, "We are not witches; we're here to help you; we are friends of El Rom." The mention of El Rom brought tears to her eyes. She moved closer to them and began to cry. Then, she asked them...

El Nina: Is he here? Can I see him?

John: No. He is not here, but he is waiting for you in ElKosia. We should escape from here; we are here to help you.

Sara opened the cell. At that time, a witch came by that side and shouted, "Who's there? Why are you opening the cell?" All four of them were frightened.

Ashkan: "It's an order from the queen to bring her."

Sara: (in a low voice) There's no queen here, you idiot.

Ashkan: Oops! My bad.

Witch: TheQueen? Which Queen?

Ashkan: Yeah, you are correct, WITCH QUEEN. You are absolutely correct. Brilliant girl…

Sara: Shut up, you dummy.

The witch approached them. John swiftly retrieved the magic liquid from his pocket and splashed it on her, envisioning El Nina's face. Instantly, the witch transformed into an exact likeness of El Nina. They confined the witch in the cell and departed. They knew the transformation would last only a day, but it provided them enough time to find a secure refuge before anyone noticed.

Sara disguised El Nina as a witch, and the four of them departed. On their journey, another witch spotted them and beckoned Sara over. The witch inquired about their destination. Sara calmly replied, "They asked me to guide them to the gateway tree, so I'm accompanying them to show the way." The witch departed silently. Everyone felt relieved.

They reached the outskirts of Magicia, feeling the urgency to hurry before the witches realized Sara had left. However, what they encountered outside Magicia left them bewildered. They found the two Korpes they had stolen waiting for them. Swiftly, they mounted the Korpes and rode off.

On their journey, John noticed something remarkable. El Nina resembled Isabel, with her sharp ears and nose, possessing a beauty that reminded him of Isabel. This realization filled him with joy. After traveling a long distance, they arrived in ElKosia early in the morning. El Rom was asleep when he heard a knock at his door. Opening it, he saw El Nina standing there. He couldn't believe his eyes. It felt like a dream come true. Tears welled up in his eyes as he ran to her and embraced her tightly, unable to contain his emotions as he cried uncontrollably.

El Rom expressed, "You are my happiness, my greatest treasure. I adore you with all my heart. Since the day you left, my life has never been the same. You brought an endless smile to my face and incredible joy to my heart; everything I lost returned with you. Now that you're here again, you've brought back everything I've ever missed. I love you, Nina. I love you more than anything."

El Rom hugged John and Ashkan with tears. He asked about everything. They told him what happened.

John: "You should leave this place. The witches will soon discover El Nina's presence here and come for her. Leave now and return after three months. Stay hidden until then." Addressing Sara, he continued, "Sara, I need you to stay with them and help keep them safe. I will return with Isabel. I promise. Until then, take care."

Everyone agreed to John's plan and departed ElKosia. John and Ashkan resumed their journey on the Korpes, taking a longer route to avoid entering

Magicia. After traveling a considerable distance, they reached their destination and kept the Korpes with them.

It was nearing the night of the full moon. John and Ashkan were resting in their tents when John suddenly heard a voice calling out to him, "Ethan, wake up." Startled, he jumped from his bed and looked around, seeing the dark sky illuminated by the full moon. He quickly woke Ashkan and grabbed the sword. Together, they hurried towards the direction of the magic tree.

As they approached, they witnessed the magic tree glowing with an awe-inspiring radiance. The tree was a breathtaking sight, adorned with fruits in various vibrant colors.

Ashkan pondered which of the fruits might contain the key. He shared his thoughts with John, who reminded him of the clue they had: "Only the one with a colorful heart can find the magic tree." John speculated that the key might be in the fruit with 3–4 colors.

John instructed Ashkan to hold onto the sword while he climbed the tree himself. As John approached the tree, he began to hear eerie voices in the vicinity.

Just as they approached, creatures resembling wolves with long nails and wings emerged from the tree, their heads conspicuously absent. John and Ashkan were gripped with fear at the horrifying sight. Reacting swiftly, Ashkan tossed the sword to John, who drew his knife. Together, they bravely confronted the creatures.

The magic sword proved formidable, driving the creatures to flee in fear. Despite sustaining numerous wounds, John pressed on, driven by determination.

Ignoring his injuries, John ascended the tree, nearing the fruit with careful determination. With just inches separating him from plucking the fruit, the entire tree suddenly vanished before his eyes. He plummeted to the ground, but the branches of another tree broke his fall, leaving him bruised but not severely injured.

Ashkan gently carried John in his arms and quickly gathered ingredients to make medicines from the resources nearby. John remained unconscious for three days, deeply troubled upon waking. He sobbed, "I lost her in my world, and I will lose her here too. I don't think I'll ever have her back."

Ashkan comforted him with reassuring words, saying, "No matter what happens, we keep trying until the end. We have nothing to lose."

Ashkan felt sorrowful seeing John's wounds. He mentioned the Heart Lake, rumored to have waters that could heal injuries swiftly. However, reaching it required crossing Giacia, the land of giants. He asked John if he wanted to undertake the journey, but John declined.

"No, I'll be fine," John replied. "The only pain that matters to me is the one I've carried all these years. No lake or magic can heal that."

After days of training, John and Ashkan began their vigil, eagerly awaiting the arrival of the wolf-like creatures on the day of the full moon. To their surprise, large snakes with legs emerged from the tree instead. Unfazed, they fought bravely and managed to defeat all of the creatures.

John quickly ascended the tree and plucked a fruit. Upon cutting it open with his sword, they found no key inside. Disappointed, they witnessed the tree disappearing once more.

John dropped the knife to the ground and knelt. Meanwhile, Ashkan noticed the handle of the sword slowly opening. They both watched eagerly as the handle revealed itself to be the key. The fruit had merely served as a password to unlock the sword. This discovery filled them with hope.

The key had a clue inscribed on it: "The one with the big heart can find the temple."

Ashkan: I know you can do this. I know you will understand the clue; you are really brave and intelligent, like your father. How can a genius man not have a son like you?

John felt worthy. John knew what the clue meant. John asked Ashkan to leave.

John: This journey is going to be more dangerous than before, and I can't risk your life for this.

Ashkan: Wait. You know where the temple is.

John: Yes. This clue says about the heart lake you've mentioned. I should do this by myself.

Ashkan: No, I won't let you do that.

John: You have to. Now you have a lady waiting for you, and you should find Sara. If I don't come back, you should look after her; she's just a girl. I know she will be safe and happy with you. Do this for me, Ashkan, please.

John urged Ashkan to leave. As Ashkan departed, John felt a pang of longing, realizing he might never see his good friend again. Ashkan had been more than just a friend; he was a selfless companion who had been willing to sacrifice his life for John. Without Ashkan's steadfast support, John doubted he would have come this far. They had shared a bond like brothers, and John deeply cherished their time together.

While walking, John noticed the surroundings becoming increasingly daunting. He came across a massive footprint that was as large as himself, realizing the enormity of the giants. Despite his fear, he pressed onward. The trees grew larger as he advanced, towering so high that their tops seemed to touch the sky. These colossal trees bore fruits that were incredibly oversized, some even four times larger than John himself lying on the ground. He observed enormous houses but curiously saw no giants in sight.

Walking onward, John suddenly heard a noise that grew louder as it approached him. He swiftly ran and sought refuge under a small cave. The giants arrived and settled close to the rock where John hid. Trembling with fear, John dared not move as one of the giants came uncomfortably close to his hiding place.

Then, they heard a distant sound. All the giants abruptly stood up and headed toward the source of the noise. Taking advantage of the distraction, John hurriedly emerged from his hiding place and saw Ashkan running towards him.

"I told you to leave; it's too dangerous," John pleaded.

"How could I leave you alone? I promised I'd stand by you no matter what," Ashkan insisted.

Near a large tree, a giant devouring fruit noticed them. John and Ashkan bolted as the giant gave chase. During their escape, John slipped on a rope and fell. Ashkan rushed back to help, but the giant closed in fast. Urging John to flee, Ashkan stayed behind. John sprinted away, but when he glanced back, Ashkan hadn't moved. Calling out desperately, John heard Ashkan say, "Please go, find your love, find her for me." Before John could reach him, the giant snatched Ashkan in its hand and crushed him like an insect.

John fled, tears streaming down his face. The giant's teeth were stained with his blood as he made his escape from Giacia. The giants remained trapped within Giacia due to a curse placed upon them by the witches.

John wept bitterly, his heart heavy with thoughts of his brother Ashkan. Looking up at the sky, he whispered, "I will miss you, brother. Your hearty laugh, your wise words—always there when I needed help. I'll miss your hugs, they made everything better. Your selflessness, dropping everything to help those you cared about. Our talks, from important matters to the most obscure topics."

"I promise to find Isabel," he continued through tears, "and show her a star, saying 'That's my brother, who sacrificed his life for me to find you.'"

The next day, John embarked on his quest to find Heart Lake. Overwhelmed with grief from losing Ashkan, John couldn't stop crying. When he finally reached Heart Lake, he found no temple there. Devastated, John felt defeated. He questioned the purpose of all his struggles and sacrifices, including losing Ashkan and enduring so many difficult days. Hopelessness consumed him.

Suddenly, John heard a voice that seemed like Ashkan's. "John, you are incredibly brave, intelligent, and smart. Your father must be so proud of you. Use your intellect," the voice encouraged. However, John found himself unable to focus or think clearly.

Out of anger, John threw the key into the lake and knelt on the ground. Suddenly, all the water in the lake dried up, and in no time the lake was empty. John stood up and went to check, wiping his tears. He saw the temple. Yes, the temple was under the lake, the temple of King Poseedios. John became really happy and felt great. He opened the temple with the key and ran inside the temple to see mountains of gold and much more. He went searching for the statue and found it near a golden pillar. He walked to it, held the hands of the statue, and closed his eyes. He knew what he was going to wish for. He thought of her; he thought about her being alive; he wished for her. He opened his eyes, but nothing had happened.

John suddenly noticed the face of the statue. It resembled Ashkan, and beneath it was inscribed a name: "King PoseediosFardobe." John couldn't believe his eyes. Was Ashkan King Poseedios? Or was the king a relative of his? His mind raced with uncertainty. How could this be possible, he wondered? Perhaps King Poseedios had never died, and perhaps he never would.

Suddenly, he heard a call from behind, "Ethan." John turned around with tears flooding his eyes, searching for the source of the voice. It was Isabel. His eyes welled up with tears of joy, and his lips stretched into a wide smile. It had been a long time since he had felt such happiness. He watched as she ran towards him. John walked towards her, smiling and crying simultaneously.

Suddenly, he stumbled and fell—plunging into a deep pit.

John opened his eyes, and a doctor came to him.

Doctor: Hey…Welcome back Ryan

It hurts when you wake up from a dream where you were with them.

PART 2

ALL ABOUT A DREAM

JOHN KINGSTON IN DREAM WORLD

EVERY GOOD THING STARTS WITH A DREAM AND SOME GOOD THINGS STILL REMAIN AS A DREAM

TIME 6:28

John woke up from a nightmare he saw last night.

Suddenly, he got ready and went to school. During class, someone called him "John Alfred Kingston." It was the janitor who came to escort John to the principal's office. For a moment, John was taken aback, fearing he might be reprimanded for his low exam scores.

As he entered the principal's office, John was surprised to see Isabel seated there— the girl he loved most. His anxiety increased; he dreaded the possibility of being humiliated in front of her. However, to his astonishment, the principal congratulated him for being the best football player and sports champion of the year. The principal's words filled John with immense pride, especially knowing Isabel had heard it all. It meant a great deal to him, and he returned home that day with a heart full of happiness.

While closing the gate of his house, he caught sight of Isabel again, just a few feet away. They were neighbors, separated only by a few walls.

At night, John took his phone and scrolled through Isabel's pictures, slowly drifting off to sleep.

Suddenly, John woke up shivering from the cold, feeling disoriented. He fell down and struggled to his feet, noticing that everything around him had changed—windows were broken, dust filled the air, and darkness engulfed his room like a haunted house.

Feeling uneasy, John ventured outside and searched for his father, but found no one. He briefly questioned if he was still dreaming, but the vividness of his surroundings felt all too real. His home felt eerily deserted, adding to his sense of dread.

In the distance, John spotted a blinking red light that unnerved him further. Fearful, he retreated to his room, trying to convince himself that it was all just a dream. He lay back down on his bed and eventually drifted back to sleep.

The next morning, John woke up feeling relieved that everything seemed normal again. He dismissed the events of the previous night as "stupid nightmares!" and proceeded with his usual routine of getting ready for school.

At school, John shared the bizarre experience with his best friend Benjamin. To their surprise, Benjamin had also encountered a similar situation the previous night. Both of them were intrigued by this coincidence. John joked that it must be their bond, and Benjamin laughed along with him.

That night, John felt a slight fear. It was the first time in his life he prayed before going to sleep. Surprisingly, nothing unusual happened that night. This pattern continued for several days—no nightmares, no encounters with haunted places—everything was calm and normal. Benjamin also went through days without experiencing anything strange.

As time passed, the days turned into weeks, and both John and Ben enjoyed a respite from their unsettling experiences.

One day, as heavy rain poured down, John arrived home after school to find it empty. He learned that his grandmother had been hospitalized, and everyone had gone to be with her. John decided to spend the night at Benjamin's house instead. They passed the time playing games and sharing spooky stories until they eventually went to sleep.

In the middle of the night, both John and Benjamin woke up to the same sensation of shivering, darkness, and eerie sounds. Curious and emboldened by each other's presence, they ventured outside to explore. Despite the unsettling atmosphere, being together gave them courage, and they enjoyed their adventure, exploring every corner of the village.

Suddenly, they noticed a red light blinking erratically, almost as if it were about to go out. Satisfied with their explorations, they returned to Benjamin's house and went back to sleep.

The next day, John shared his experience of the previous night, and Benjamin casually remarked, "Wasn't our adventure nice?" John was puzzled. "You had the same experience?" he asked. Benjamin explained that it wasn't just a dream or a nightmare; it might be a dream world where only they existed. He mentioned seeing something that said, "If someone writes the numbers 690452 on their wrist before sleep, they might be trapped in their dream or a parallel universe forever. Perhaps that's what happened to us. I believe we were exploring this dream world all night."

Despite feeling a bit scared, John agreed with Benjamin's perspective. They continued sleeping together for many days to enjoy their shared dream world during their study sessions. John expressed his wish for Isabel to join them in the dream world, but Benjamin cautioned him against it, saying it would be painful to wake up from a dream where she was with them.

One day, John returned to his own house with excitement because the next day was Isabel's birthday, February 7th. He eagerly sent her a birthday wish at midnight, a tradition he followed every year. He had bought a beautiful gift for her and drifted off to sleep, imagining her reaction to the gift.

After a while, John woke up and found himself back in the dream world, completely forgetting about his plans for Isabel's birthday. He decided to visit Benjamin's house, but to his surprise, Ben was nowhere

to be found. Perplexed, John turned back and noticed a house that didn't exist in his real world.

It was raining heavily as John approached the house, illuminated by flashes of lightning. He called out loudly, "Bennn... bennnyyyy," hearing footsteps inside. With each step, his fear mounted. Entering a room, he suddenly found himself locked inside. Panic rising, he cried out for help, searching desperately for another way out. As he emerged through another door, a dark shadow lunged at him with a deafening roar, rendering John unconscious.

When he woke, he fled from the house in terror, only to realize the red light was no longer visible. Fear gripped him as he ran, but his house was nowhere to be found. The surroundings felt eerily empty, engulfed by the storm's fury and John's mounting dread. Alone and uncertain, he struggled to grasp what was happening and what he should do next.

John searched Benjamin's house thoroughly, but there was no sign of him. Desperate and feeling trapped, he climbed to the top of the house where he had seen the red light. Hoping to return to reality by sleeping when the light flashed again, he decided to rest.

Hours later, John woke up, only to realize he was still in the same eerie dream world. The realization sank in—he was cursed to remain there, devoid of day and night, alone with the unsettling mysteries and horrors of the place. He mourned the loss of his normal life, yearning to see his parents and Isabel again. John felt a deep ache knowing he couldn't give Isabel the gift he had carefully chosen for her.

John wandered aimlessly, eventually finding himself near Isabel's house. Overwhelmed with emotions, he decided to sit and gather his thoughts. Suddenly, footsteps approached him from behind. When he turned, he saw a girl whose face was obscured in the darkness.

"Alfiee...?" she called out, using the nickname only Isabel had ever used for him. John's heart leaped with hope. As the girl emerged from the shadows, he saw Isabel's beautiful face, and his happiness was indescribable, like that of a child reunited with a lost treasure.

She approached him and suddenly collapsed unconscious. John quickly moved to support her, then attempted to locate water to revive her, but none was available. After a few tense minutes, she regained consciousness and slowly opened her eyes.

"Alfie, where have you been? Where is Benjamin?" Isabel asked. John didn't know how to answer; he kept silent and continued looking at her. "You both have been missing for 3 days; your parents and our whole school are very upset about your absence. What is this place? Am I dreaming? Or is it all real? I don't understand anything. What is happening to me? How did I get here? I'm so scared. Are you both hiding here? John was shaken. What? We both? Is Ben also missing?

Is he not there? No, he is also missing. That's when John understood Ben was also trapped there. "What's happening here, Alfie? I don't understand anything,"

Isabel said, bewildered. John explained everything to Isabel. She was shocked. "I can't believe this. I think I'm losing my mind. If Ben is not here and not there, then where must he be?" John asked. "I should go and find him. I know he is here."

Isabel didn't let him go alone; she insisted on accompanying him. They began their search together. During their walk, Isabel asked him about how she could go back to the real world. John reassured her, "Don't worry; you will be back in the real world when you wake up."

"Oh! Then why can't you come back?" Isabel questioned. John smiled at her and said, "I don't know."

Then she decided to ask him about his crush on her. She told him, "I heard you have a big crush on me. Is that true?" John was a little bit shy. But John opened his heart. He had loved her since 7th grade.

Every time he looks at her without her knowing, or when she's absent from school, he becomes very sad that day. She was the light upon which he fell and the flower upon which he prayed. She was his everything, even though she never noticed him back. He loved her with all his heart and found solace in her smile. He dreamed of living with her, smiling with her, growing old with her, and eventually dying with her.

John told her how much he had loved her all these years. Isabel was really impressed, a light smile on her face revealing her happiness, because she loved him back. John saw her beautiful smile and told her, "I love the way you smile with your crooked teeth." They laughed together. They searched for Ben for some time, but they couldn't find him. John took her back to her house and asked her to go to sleep. Thus, the day passed.

The next day, at the same time, John waited hopefully for Isabel in front of her house. She came outside, this time with a smile on her face. John was captivated by her smile. He told her, "I think the real world lost the moon because the moon is now here." Isabel smiled lovingly at him. They continued searching for Benjamin together. This time, they joked, argued, and gradually grew closer to each other. John said to her, "I had a gift for you that I meant to give you on your birthday." Isabel replied, "Don't worry, Alfie. I took it from your room yesterday and left a thank-you note on your table. I knew it was meant for me."

And that day also passed without finding Ben; at times, they forgot about him as they enjoyed each other's company.

The next day when she came, they resumed their search for Ben. They looked almost everywhere, and it grew late enough that Isabel wanted to return home. John pleaded with her to stay. Despite her fear, she cherished this dream world and being with him. John knew that if she didn't return to sleep before the red light blinked, she might be stuck forever. Yet, he yearned for her company.

For that reason, he didn't mention anything about it; he understood it was wrong, and he felt deeply sorry for it, but his love for her was immense. He cherished their time together, their banter, and their laughter. It was the most difficult decision he had ever made in his life.

They traveled a lot, and they both got tired. They searched more places for him, but they couldn't find Ben. Isabel decided to go back. John knew that she couldn't go back but said nothing. When she reached her house, she couldn't see it there. She was very upset and returned to John. She cried and hugged John. He was both sad and happy at the same time; he held her tight and looked at her face, and Isabel could see a lot of love and care in his eyes. He comforted her by saying that he's with her always and forever.

What do we do now, Alfie? Is there any way I can go back to the real world?" John looked at her with sadness. He regretted his decision but remained silent, choosing instead to comfort her.

After a while, they realized they hadn't found Benjamin. Over the past few days, they had searched everywhere except for the horror house where John was trapped on Isabel's birthday. John told Isabel about the house, and though she knew he was afraid to go there, she was courageous enough to suggest they check it. She insisted that if Benjamin was there and needed their help, they should go and assist him. Together, they entered the horror house. The place was terrifying, with strange noises emanating from within. John was visibly afraid, but Isabel held his hand tightly. As they entered, the main door closed behind them. John started trembling and asked timidly, 'Can we please go back?' Isabel squeezed his hand reassuringly and urged him, 'Never give up on your best friend.' They pressed forward, calling Benjamin's name loudly.

They heard screaming from upstairs. They ran towards the sound and saw someone on the ground, crying for help. They thought it was Benjamin, but as they got closer, it wasn't him; it was a girl. She was so scared and tired that they helped her and came out of that house. Her innocent face told about her loneliness and how she felt relief after seeing them. She said she was trapped in that house for 2 days, and they asked more about how she came here and her whereabouts. At first, she couldn't answer anything. After a while, she started to talk. She said her name was Sara.

She and her parents were traveling on a ship to the USA, and suddenly their ship fell into a whirlpool. She doesn't know what happened then. When she opened her eyes, she was here. She said one thing too: "There was a man with me on that ship who looked like you." She pointed to John. "He played with me on the ship, and he was the only man who stayed with me while everyone else on the ship left. Even my parents didn't care about me at that time. I think they saved themselves, but this man took me from my room and hugged me tightly. And I was younger when I last remembered. I don't really understand what's happening here." She again started to cry.

They all became so confused because none of it made sense. How could she have come here from a ship, and who was the person she was talking about? Everything they believed and thought was wrong. It's not just a dream world, then what is it? John started to think about all of this. Then they decided to build a tent. They collected the needed things and clothes to make it. Sara also accompanied them. The three of them wanted to escape from there. They noticed one thing: they hadn't eaten anything since last week. They realized that here they weren't feeling any hunger or thirst. Then what is this place? Is this a dream or a nightmare? Isabel asked. That day, too, passed. The question remained unanswered.

John couldn't sleep, thinking about his best friend Ben. He began to worry: what if something happens to him? No, he is so brave and clever that he will escape from any trouble very easily.

The next day, somebody knocked at the door of the tent. John opened the door. He was surprised to see Benjamin. His eyes were filled with tears, and they hugged. John asked, Ben, where have you been? We searched for you everywhere for the last few days. I was searching for the way out from here. I traveled a long distance. They both entered the tent, and Ben could see Isabel and Sara. Why is Isabel here? And who is this? Ben asked. This is Sara. Isabel and Sara are also trapped here like us, but Sara's story is different. John explained her story to Benjamin.

As per Isabel, we are absent from the real world now, which means if we die here, we are dead in the real world too. But don't worry, I have found a way to escape from here. I have seen a red light at the top of a building, maybe a research center, lab, or something. There are so many buildings there. I think there will be people there, and we can seek their help. If we reach there, we can go back to our home world. They packed so many things that would be useful for their journey. They started their journey. Ben took them to a tall building to show them what he saw.

They could see many buildings in the distance, and they decided to head towards them. However, reaching there would involve overcoming some challenges; they could see something flowing in black color, likely a river, and a large wall surrounding the buildings. Leaving the building, they resumed their journey. At that moment, they sensed something unusual happening. The sky turned grey, lightning flashed, and thunder roared, unsettling them slightly. Despite their fear, they pressed onward. Suddenly, a shadow appeared out of nowhere and enveloped them. They could see nothing but flashes of light before all of them fell unconscious.

After some time, they opened their eyes and realized that Sara was missing. They called her name loudly as they searched everywhere. Benjamin felt very sad because he had already started to like her, despite her being a stranger. They searched for her for a long time. Suddenly, they heard a loud noise, and everything began to shake. Looking around, they saw the whole land trembling. They had no idea what was happening. Ben climbed to the top of another building and saw something unexpected: their world was about to be destroyed. Ben quickly ran outside and urged them to escape from there as soon as possible.

The three of them ran towards that place. They reached the black river, which looked like tar and fog were coming out of it. There was no way to cross it. John and Ben decided to make a boat. They took everything they saw nearby, tied it together, and made a raft. After a very hard effort, they finally made it. Nobody was sure enough that it could carry all of them and reach the other side. But they have no other choices. Anyway, they got onto the raft.

Isabel was really afraid. John held her tight and said, "Don't worry; nothing is going to happen to you." Ben was leading the raft. Suddenly, the black water started to flow swiftly, so John also accompanied Ben. They approached the other side. John came out of the raft first, then Isabel and Ben tried to come out, but at that moment, the flow became heavy, and the boat was destroyed. Both of them fell into the water. They tried to cling to a tree. John rushed near them, even though Ben was closer to him; he tried to save Isabel first. He pulled her onto the land and comforted her with a hug. When he went back for Ben, it was heartbreaking to see Ben being carried away by the black water. John screamed, "Ben!"

John couldn't handle it, so he started to cry. Isabel went to him and hugged him; both of them cried a lot. John was literally broken. But Isabel could see that their world was going to end. So, she held John's hand, and they ran. They reached in front of the giant wall. They looked around and searched everywhere, but they couldn't find a door or an entrance to enter.

John sat there on his knees and started to cry again. "How cheating I am." He grabbed Isabel's hands and told her, "I'm so sorry, Isa. I'm not a good friend or even a good person. I don't have any humanity; I'm a monster. That's why I let my brother die, no! I killed him. I don't deserve any mercy." Isabel told him, "Why are you saying this? You didn't do anything, then why are you saying this all?" Isabel tried to comfort him. But it didn't help, and John revealed the truth.

He said, "I betrayed you too. I can't hold that anymore." Isabel asked, "What have you done, Alfie? Tell me."

"I know that you can't go back home forever if you don't go back to sleep before the red light goes off. I deliberately hid the truth from you because I need you with me. That much, I love you. I'm so sorry, Isa."

Isabel was extremely shocked. She let go of his hands and cried. "How could you do that to me? You betrayed me. I'm here because of you. I'm going to die because of you. I am never going to forgive you for this."

John walked near her to explain, but she didn't listen.

After some time, John went near the wall. The wall opened automatically, and a voice came from inside: "Welcome, Mr. John Kingston." They both were surprised at how well it knew his name. They both entered; it was a fabulous and big place full of buildings and machines. They called out loudly, "Hello, is anybody there?" But there was no response. They could see so many rooms there that they entered all of them. They could only see machines and some research things there. They couldn't find any people there. Isabel didn't even speak a single word to John. That made John very depressed. They both wandered around there and couldn't find anything. At last, they saw a room that looked different from the others.

They came in front of that room. They were surprised by what they saw because on the door of that room, there was a "Property of Kingston" board, but John had no idea what it was all about. They entered the room; it was the control room of that building. Through the glass, they could see a big machine in front of them. They saw a computer in the room, and John opened it. Luckily for them, it still worked. They checked it and saw some videos on it. John opened the first video, and a man said, "Hi, my name is John Ethan Kingston, and this is Project Isa..." John paused the video. Isabel asked him, "Why does he look like you? Is that your future self?""I don't know; I don't understand any of this."

John played the rest of the video: "…bel, it's all set up, and everyone is ready for this. I'm so excited to see my love once again, and I hope God makes this happen." After that, the man showed a photo, and John paused the video again.

"It's me, Isabel. How is that even possible? I don't understand anything. This is insane." Isabel started to cry.

John tried to calm her, but she shouted at him, "Don't touch me. You are the reason for all this."

Then John opened the next video. In that video, the man was crying. "My name is John Ethan Kingston, and this is my last project, 'Project I.' I know this project is insane, but I have to do it. I'm doing this for my love because I can't live without her. It's been 10 years since she left me. She died because of me; I probably killed her."

"It was February 7th, 2019—her birthday. I planned a surprise party for her at the hotel, but because of some issues in my lab, I forgot about everything. She tried to call me so many times, but I ignored her. Finally, after multiple calls, I answered and shouted at her."

That was the first and only time I had ever shouted at her. I forgot about everything; I forgot it was her birthday. She got scared of my behavior and decided to come to me. An hour later, I got a call from the hospital, and I could not forgive myself for that. She was the only person who saw me when I was invisible. I can't live without her; that's why I am creating this world.

This machine will take me to the past, where Isabel is alive, and it will create a new world in her dream for us where we can live for eternity. There will be only me, and Isabel is going to be there. There will be no hunger or thirst, no aging; my love and I will live forever and ever. It's been 10 years since she left; time is moving so fast. I hate time; time is the biggest enemy of humankind. No one can do anything about it, but I can control it.

Time is a curse.

Time is humanity's biggest enemy.

Time makes us young and old.

Time makes us old and ugly.

Time takes us to death.

Every second, we are close to death.
Time is an ugly gift that everyone has.
But no one can reverse it.
No one can control it.
But can choose how to spend it.
Even though we spend our time perfectly
Time will kill us one day. No!
Time is killing us every day.
Time is a curse.
That's why it's priceless.
The one thing that money can't buy

Suddenly a pop-up message appeared with a timer, indicating that "Project I" was going to end in 45 minutes. John said to Isabel, "This is going to end. We should find a way to get out of here." Then John opened the next video. Ethan said, "Once I get into that world, I can only escape through a portal, but I made that for her; if she ever wanted to get out of there, she could use that. Only one person can go through that portal. And if anything goes wrong, this place will self-destruct in 50 days."

John said, "We have to find out how to open the portal; we must find out. We don't have much time." Isabel took the mouse and opened the last video. It was security camera footage. Everyone was running around.

The danger alarm was ringing, and there was Ethan on his knees, crying. The machine was going to explode.

Then a man came and took Ethan with him.

"Alfie... What is this? I don't understand," Isabel said.

"But I did, Isa. This is me from another universe, and that girl is you. They also loved each other like we did. He tried to make another world to live in with her because she died. She died because of him, and that regret made him do that, and he failed. It was meant for Ethan's Isabel, but it came to my Isabel. That was the mistake that happened that day. That's why we are here. I created this world from another universe, and I'm the reason for all of this."

That man loved Isabel so much that he would do anything to live with her, just like I did for you. He loved her so much that he would die for her, just like me. I am so sorry, Isa. I dragged you into this because I love you more than anything in the world. I think it's my fate to fall in love with you in every universe and lose you in every universe. But if there is another life, I wish we could live together. Please forgive me, Isa.

He said, "Don't you remember about the portal? We have to find it. John took her hand and ran over to the machine, checking all around. He found a blue button and figured that this must be it. He tried to press it, but Isabel stopped him and said, "Wait, Alfie, it can only carry one. Yeah, it'll be you, Isa; you shouldn't be here. You're here because of me. I can't let you die with me; you should go through it." John pressed the button.

The portal opened in front of the machine. At that moment, the alarm started ringing. John hugged Isabel and said, "We don't have much time. Hurry, my love. I'm so happy for you. I'm so glad I spent some days with you. Those memories are enough for me. I think I found you in another universe; that's why I lost you in this. Thank you for loving me, Isa." John slightly pushed her toward the portal, and she walked slowly toward it with tears. Then she stopped, turned back, and looked at John. She ran to him and kissed him.

"I can't leave you here; I can't leave you to die alone. I'm coming with you; we can die together." John looked into her eyes and said goodbye, love. He pushed her into the portal, and she disappeared. John dropped to his knees and screamed. He heard a whisper in his ear, "Ethan." Suddenly, the place vanished completely.

Everything has an end.

My world just ended.

I feel lost inside.

I feel broken inside.

But I loved her.

I lived for her.

I died for her.

Her smile stays.

Her memories stay.

But I have lost everything now.

Because she was my everything.

But I kept whispering.

Maybe in my next life.

Maybe in my next life.

John opened his eyes, and a doctor came to him.

Doctor: Hey…Welcome back Ryan

I WISH YOU WEREN'T MY INCOMPLETE WISH

PART 3

ALL ABOUT THE ZORM DREAM

JOHN KINGSTON ZORM APOCALYPSE

OUR STORY NEVER STARTED SO THERE WILL BE NO ENDING

TIME 6:29

John woke up hearing his niece's voice.

Only 7 days left for his wedding. John took the wedding card from the table with a smile. "John Mikael Kingston weds Isabel," he read aloud, smiling at it once again. It had been his dream for so many years. John had loved Isabel for half of his life.

Isabel was his neighbor. He fell in love with her 13 years ago, and now he is going to marry her. John proposed to her so many times and got rejected every single time because Isabel was afraid of relationships.

Suddenly, he heard the sound of many police vehicles, and from one of them, he heard an announcement. "Announcement for everyone in this area: do not leave your homes; close your doors securely; remain indoors until further notice." John hurried downstairs and turned on the TV. It reported, "A new virus has emerged from a deer and has become highly dangerous, spreading rapidly. A family encountered a deer sleeping near a road while traveling through the forest. When they tried to capture it, the deer bit one of them, spreading the virus. The infected individual began exhibiting strange behavior, prompting hospitalization, where the virus has now spread. This virus is named Zormus. Infected individuals are termed Zorms, similar to zombies. Everyone should secure their homes and protect themselves."

Everyone became scared after hearing this. John went outside to assess the situation; there were soldiers everywhere, armed with weapons. John called Isabel on the phone.

Isabel: Mike what's happening here. We are scared.

John: Don't worry, Isa; it's going to be ok soon. Shut all the doors carefully, ok? Don't come out.

Isabel: How long will it take?

John: I don't know. They said on the news that the virus is like zombies; it spreads through bites. I hope everything will be alright soon.

Isabel: What about our wedding, Mike? There are only 7 days left.

John: Don't worry about it now. We've waited for so long. Just hold on for a few more days.

John ended the call and asked God, "Why are you always against me? How could you do this to me? I prayed for her every single day to you, and you almost gave her to me, and now this."

John and Isabel were childhood friends, and John fell in love with her when he was in 7th grade. Years passed, and every time he opened his heart to her, it turned out to be a broken one.

One day, he decided to propose to her again for the last and final time. He prepared something to tell her. At that time, she was studying in another state, so he waited for her to come home. One day, her college closed for a week, and she returned. John decided to confess his feelings to her. He sent her a message and asked her to come to his house. The next day, when she arrived, John was well prepared, but he couldn't say anything that he had planned to tell her. It left him feeling sad.

Isabel: Why did you call me? Is there any problem?

John: No problem. I just want to tell you something.

Isabel: Stop! I already know what you're going to say. I've told you so many times that I can't love you. I'm scared of my parents. How many times do I have to repeat this? Don't you feel ashamed for always begging me to love you back? Stop it, and move on. It's never going to happen. I can't love someone like you, and you're my neighbor too. How many times do you have to repeat the same thing? I'm tired of it. Look at us; we're not meant to be together; that's why God made us neighbors. Please leave me alone. I'm begging you, please. And one more thing: don't think I secretly love you. I don't like people who wear glasses.

John stood like a stone. Her words hit him hard. He couldn't respond. He felt like his world was ending. Not a single tear fell from his eyes. Her words pierced his heart, leaving him frightened to the core.

Today I woke up with a scar on my heart.
And it hurts.
I got that scar so long ago.
But it hurts more today.
I begged her to stay with me.
But she left.
Left me without saying goodbye.
Left me with a scar.
That will hurt until I die.
She told me that she had to go.
All I can say is don't leave.
But she left me.
Our distance is not so far.
But it felt like miles.
One day I will be smiling at you.
From the sky with the stars

Isabel felt regretful for hurting John so deeply. She hadn't intended to say so much to him, but it had slipped out. She decided to apologize and went to his house, but John wasn't there. No one knew where he had gone. His mother was distraught and crying, which scared Isabel even more. She thought, "Is he going to commit suicide or something?" and became increasingly anxious. She tried calling him, but he didn't answer.

She tried again and again, but still received no response.

John was on a mountain, thinking about Isabel's words that had hurt him so badly. He decided to end his life. He thought that would make her happy. He decided to jump from the top of the mountain. Before doing so, he took his phone to look at Isabel's picture one last time. That's when he saw Isabel calling him. He answered her call. She was crying loudly. She said, "I'm so sorry, Mike. Please come back to me. We are scared. Please come back. I'm so sorry for what I said yesterday; I didn't mean that. We are all waiting for you to come back to us." Isabel's voice changed his mind, and he decided to return.

He acted like nothing had happened and went trekking. Isabel came and hugged him, asking why he did that. "Are you crazy? You love me that much?" John replied, "I have loved you for almost 8 years now. I would die for you, Isa. I love you that much. Why can't you see my love? It's clearly in my eyes, in my voice, and in my heart. But you're not seeing it. Sometimes I think maybe someone cursed me or something, and that's why you're not accepting me. Sometimes I think I'm the curse, and that's why things are like this. I don't know how to make you love me. I don't have any energy left to do that. I'm tired, and I'm done. I'm done trying to make you mine. I'm done becoming a fool, and I'm done running after you because I'm so exhausted, I feel drained of everything. Trying to prove my love, showing how much I care, spending every night thinking that tomorrow I'll get a positive reply from you. You're right, how can someone as beautiful and perfect as you love someone wearing glasses and looking like a mess? I'm done trying to make you mine, and I don't intend to force you to love me. I can't do anything anymore. I've lost all my self-respect because of you. I thought the worst you could say was no, but just think about what you said yesterday. Just imagine someone you love the most saying this to you. It will haunt you until your death. It was that deep. I don't think I can ever forget that. I'm so sorry for loving you. I wish I had never seen you because it hurts more than you think. I wish there was a painkiller for the pain in our hearts too, and I wish you weren't my unfulfilled wish." Without letting him finish, Isabel kissed John. That's how everything started.

From that day on, he began working hard for her. He needed a good job to win her over, so he studied diligently and achieved his goal.

But there was a problem. Her father didn't approve of their relationship. Isabel informed her father about their relationship, and he was displeased. He insisted that it was not going to happen. Isabel conveyed this to John. The next day, John went to her house. He pleaded earnestly in front of her father for her. John said, "I have loved your daughter since I was in 7th grade. It's been 12 years now, and I'm still deeply in love with her. She loves me too. I'm confident you won't find anyone who loves your daughter more than I do. Maybe I could live without her, but I don't want to. Maybe I could love someone else, but I don't want to love anyone else. I'm not promising to be with her for a hundred years, but I want to spend the rest of my life with her. I will make her the happiest woman, and I want to give her the love she deserves. Don't you want your daughter's happiness? I'm begging you, please give her to me. I don't want anything else, just her. Just her..."

At last, her father agreed to their marriage. They set the date for February 7th, 2019. Everything was perfect and ready, but as if fate was testing them, this happened.

He cursed his own fate. He didn't know what would happen next. John has a brother who is married and has a young daughter named Lily. Fortunately, everyone was at the house when this happened. His brother and family had come from another place for his marriage.

John and his brother James locked all the doors and placed heavy objects behind them. Little Lily became frightened watching them do these things, but her mother calmed her down. Days passed, and the virus continued to spread. It was now February 7th. John called Isabel.

John: Today is the day, don't you remember?

Isabel started to cry.

Isabel: How can I forget? I wish things would be different and normal.

John: Me too! But don't worry, go and wear your wedding dress. Go fast; I will wear mine too.

Isabel: what? Why?

John: Just go, Isa.

Both of them wore their wedding dresses.

John: We are going to get married over the phone. Are you ready?

Isabel: Ha-ha, yes, I'm ready.

John: Hey, Isabel, daughter of Martin and Elsa, will you take me as your lovely husband?

Isabel: Yes, I will. I will look after you till my last breath, and I will love you after that too. If I die before you, I will come as a ghost and still love you more.

John: ha-ha... I'm here by presenting us as husband and wife. We may now kiss each other.

Both of them laughed.

John: We are now husband and wife.

One night, they heard gunfire from outside. John looked through the windows to see what was happening and saw that the Zorms were attacking the military forces. Lily started to cry, and John took her in his arms to comfort her. After two hours, everything became completely silent. John went to the roof to investigate. He was horrified by what he saw: every soldier had turned into Zorms. There was no one left outside; everyone had turned into Zorms.

John didn't say anything to anyone except his brother. The news reported, "The Zormus virus has spread across the country, and scientists are working on finding a cure. The government will supply essential items via helicopters. Military helicopters will shoot Zorms once a week. Everyone should remain vigilant."

Months passed, and the internet connection stopped. Now John couldn't call or text Isabel. But they met each other on the roof every day.

One day, a helicopter came to provide them aid. When it dropped the supplies at Isabel's house, unfortunately, it crashed in front of their house. They had no choice but to retrieve the supplies quickly. Her father decided to do it. He cautiously looked out the window to ensure there were no Zorms nearby. Slowly, he stepped outside, grabbed the box, and hurried back. Suddenly, a Zorm appeared out of nowhere and bit him. He screamed, "Close the door!" His family was shocked by what they witnessed. Three of them burst into tears. The mother fainted, and her brother began to behave strangely, expressing a desire for revenge against the Zorms. Isabel managed to calm him down.

John didn't know what was happening. Isabel hadn't come to the roof for several days, and he waited for her anxiously. He could see the box of supplies outside their house and understood they had run out of food. He called her name loudly. She came out, and John felt saddened to see her tired and exhausted face. Isabel told him everything that had happened. John held back his tears and comforted her as best he could. He said, "Take care of your brother; he's young, and we don't know what he might do."

One day, everyone was asleep. Isabel's brother took a gun and went outside. He locked the house and started shooting at all the Zorms he saw. The loud noise attracted more Zorms, and they overwhelmed him. Isabel and her mother, exhausted from their hardships, slept through it all and didn't hear anything. The next day, they searched for him but couldn't find him. Her mother looked out the window and saw her son outside, now a Zorm. She screamed his name loudly. Isabel ran to her, and she too saw him outside. They felt utterly helpless.

Months passed. The military continued their duties. Then one day, an announcement came from a helicopter: "The scientists have found the cure for the virus. The Antizormus cure will reach you soon." They felt relieved. However, Isabel remained in pain, and it seemed never-ending.

It's like the waves.

It doesn't have an ending.

People leave people die.

Memories don't; memories never

It'll haunt us. It'll kill us.

It's like the sea.

So deep, like their love

So dark as their faith

Everything will be fine in the end.

Everything will end when the wave ends.

Months passed, but no cure or antivirus came. It had been a year since this ordeal began. Everyone had lost hope and was exhausted from living under these conditions. John heard his sister-in-law crying loudly.

He went downstairs to check on her. Lily was missing; they searched everywhere but couldn't find her. John looked outside and saw her standing there. She had gone out through the small door meant for the dog. John called to her in a soft voice, but she didn't hear him. He informed everyone and opened the door very carefully. He stepped outside slowly and called to Lily to come back, but she was so young and unaware of the danger.

She gave him a smile and ran ahead. John followed her but fell down on the stairs. A Zorm heard her smile and started to follow her. John saw this and rushed towards her. He knew he wouldn't reach her in time because the Zorm was so close. Just as the Zorm was about to grab her, it was shot in the head. John looked back and saw his best friend Benjamin in an off-road jeep. John grabbed Lily and they both got into the jeep.

Ben: The right man at the right time, ha-ha

John: Ha-ha, as always.

Ben, what are you guys doing out here?

John: Lily came out of the house through the small door, and I followed her.

Ben: You coming for a ride?

John: Oh Yeah! Drop Lily in the house, and we can go.

They went for a ride, and John noticed how everything had changed. Every building was in ruins. John saw the football field where he used to play, now destroyed. Zorms were everywhere they went, and Ben shot many of them, which saddened John because they were once normal people. John asked Ben to take him back home. They returned to his house, where Ben's presence brought happiness to everyone; Ben was like a son to them all.

Ben was the one who always stood behind John. He supported him in everything. Ben was the biggest supporter of John’s love. He was with him in every situation. Now he's also the one who saved their lives there. As he said, he is the right man at the right time.

One day, Isabel’s mother went to take a bath and noticed the window was open. She tried to close it when a Zorm grabbed her hand and bit her from outside. Now she had been bitten. She quickly locked the door from inside and called Isabel, asking her to lock the door from outside, which Isabel did. However, she didn't know why her mother had asked her to do that. After some time, Isabel heard strange noises from inside the bathroom and realized what had happened. Now she was all alone. Exhausted and despairing, everyone in her family had turned into Zorms.

Knowing Isabel was alone now, John decided to go to her and bring her to his house. His brother said, “I will come with you, John. We can do it together,” but John refused and said, "No, I will do this alone. If anything happens to me, you have to protect our family." John insisted that his brother stay behind. He prepared everything, taking two guns with him, and ventured out when there were no Zorms around. He moved slowly, avoiding making any noise.

Suddenly, Lily cried from inside Isabel's house. The sound attracted Zorms, who rushed towards the noise. John shot many of them and tried to reach Isabel's house, but he was overwhelmed by the sheer number of Zorms. They caught him just as Isabel came out of her house and hugged John. Both of them were bitten by the Zorms.

The alarm rang, and the military helicopters opened fire on everyone. Isabel and John died before they could turn into Zorms.

John opened his eyes, and a doctor came to him.

Doctor: Hey…Welcome back Ryan

Love is a promise that we give to our own hearts

PART 4

ALL ENDS WITH A DREAM

JOHN KINGSTON IN LOVE

SOME LOVE STORIES NEVER END SOME LOVE STORIES NEVER START TO END

TIME 6:30

John woke up to the sound of his car's horn.

It was a new place for him. New people, new culture, new spaces—everything was new. His parents brought him here for his happiness and to change his mind from that deep depression. He was totally lost, so his parents took him up here. They are trying to create a new atmosphere to make him forget about his pain.

John went to join his new college. Even though it was his first day, he wasn't very excited. When the teacher asked for his name, John replied, "John Robert Kingston." Some of his classmates approached him and tried to be friendly, hoping to establish a good friendship. However, he wasn't ready for that and remained silent. Others attempted to bully him, but he ignored their actions and walked away from them.

It was the first day, so the class ended by noon. John rode his bike home. Due to his depression, he had become introverted. He didn't even talk to his parents after the incident. It wasn't anger, but rather a sense of being lost. His parents were deeply disappointed by his change. His mother confided in his father, expressing concern that he was just sitting in a dark room doing nothing. His father tried to comfort her, assuring her that everything would be okay. In the past, John had been addicted to mobile phones, but now he simply hated them.

There is a large space of regret in his heart. He has something in his heart that not even he could forgive himself for what he did. He was always sitting in his room, looking at a girl's picture, and crying every day since that incident happened. He forgot how to smile; he forgot the meaning of happiness; and all he was doing was crying and crying every day, all night, thinking about her.

After a few days, in the morning, his mother entered his room to wake him up for college. John refused, saying he was not going to college that day. His mother noted that it was only the beginning of the college days. John became very rude and left the house. He took his bike and rode through the streets. Suddenly, a girl fell in front of his bike. John was shocked. He approached her and tried to help. He asked, "Are you okay?" She replied, "Yes, I'm okay." John looked into her eyes; they seemed so familiar to him. She introduced herself. "I am Lisa; may I know your good name, please?" "I am John," John replied. They met briefly and then parted ways.

John went back to his house and entered his room. He took the picture and started staring at it until he fell asleep. The next day, his mom didn't wake him. He woke up by himself and went to college, only remembering the place where he had met Lisa yesterday. He barely made it through that day at college; his mind was blank. He felt relieved to hear that college would be closing for a month due to the festival. John returned home; his mother served him food, and she became very emotional. She sat beside him and asked, "John, why aren't you talking to us? It's time to let go of her. We know that incident hurts you, but you have to stop blaming yourself; it's not your fault. We only have you. You can talk to us. We will always be with you. Why don't you understand our pain? We love you so much, John." John remained silent.

He went out, walked along the street, and reached the park. He sat on a stone bench there. A light breeze was blowing, gently touching his smooth and shiny hair. Suddenly, somebody called out, "John!" It was Lisa. A small feeling of happiness warmed his heart upon seeing her. He slowly moved his lips and replied, "Yes." She asked him, "You never smile? Why are you sitting here alone?" He replied with a simple "nothing." When she sat near him, something stirred in his heart; his heart rate increased. He recalled having this feeling before. Her face and smile seemed familiar to him.

Lisa became talkative. "I always come here at this time. It feels so nice to sit here. When I'm feeling sad, I always come here. This breeze helps calm me down. What about you? Do you usually come here?"

"No, I'm new here. I arrived just a few months ago," John replied.

"Oh, I see. Let's play a game. Will you join?" Lisa asked.

John declined, saying, "Sorry, it's too late. I need to go." He walked back home. Lisa called after him, "John, will you come tomorrow? Let's meet."

John nodded to confirm he would come and left. That night, he slept well for the first time in a long while.

Then the next day, John woke up and got ready, which was unusual. He was a little excited and waited for the evening. He didn't know what was happening to him; he felt those feelings again and was traveling to another world. In the evening, John went to the park and waited for Lisa. He waited a lot. During that time, he could see the breeze touching the leaves, and those leaves were dancing along with the breeze. The children were playing with a lot of energy. Their innocent faces made John smile, and the red sun was saying goodbye; John realized that it was getting dark. He understood that Lisa would not come, so he started to return. He was desperate. Then he heard a call from far away: "John..." He saw that Lisa was running towards him. Her beautiful face filled his heart. She asked, "Are you leaving? I thought that you would not come since it's too late." "Sorry, I was a little busy. I wanted to say something. Tomorrow onwards, the festival is starting. If you don't mind, will you join me? My parents aren't here. I and my grandmother are alone. So I need company. If you come, I will be happy."

John said, "No, I will be busy tomorrow. I will come another day." Lisa became very sad, and both left.

The next day, at the same time, Lisa came to the park and waited for John. She sat on the stone bench for a long time. But John didn't come. A week passed like this: every evening, Lisa came to the park and waited for him. Meanwhile, John was at home, staring and crying at that picture the whole night. One day, while he was sleeping, he heard a stone-slapping sound at his window. When he went to check, he saw that Lisa was waiting. Slowly, he came outside his house.

Lisa asked, "Why haven't you come to the park for the last week? Weren't you here?"

"Hey, it's nothing. I was just not feeling well," John replied.

"I have an idea that this will make all your illnesses go away. Let's go to a wonderful place. Let's go on your bike."

John was not very interested, but he agreed to go. They went to that place. To John's perfect amazement, it was a stunningly beautiful place—a magnificent waterfall, painting a colorful rainbow in the sky. Seeing this breathtaking sight, John emerged from his dark, vacuum-filled, and dull state of mind. He smiled with heartfelt joy.

Lisa asked, "So you know how to smile?" While looking into her eyes, John again fell silent for a while. There was something special in her eyes that he couldn't understand.

He sat down somewhere already. She pulled him toward the water. When he touched her, he felt a sensation like a spark. John wasn't ready to jump into the water; he was afraid of everything. Lisa jumped into the water and called him again, but she didn't force him. She understood his fear. After some time, they returned. It was raining heavily, and both of them were wet. Lisa was shivering, so she hugged John tightly from the back seat of his bike. They reached in front of John's house. John invited her inside, saying, "Let's warm up before you go. I'll drop you home." Lisa declined silently and left without a word. John was confused whether she had misunderstood him. He became tense. He never asked about her whereabouts or anything; he waited for her to explain everything. Since John didn't have a mobile phone, he had no way to contact her.

The next day, John confirmed that he would join Lisa for the festival. She was thrilled to hear this. She said, "Today is the last day of the festival. Tonight is the biggest night in this village. The villagers don't sleep on this night. Everyone will be busy dancing, playing games, and enjoying themselves. I'm sure this will be a memorable day in your life."

At night, they both went to the festival. They saw many interesting games there. Lisa took John to a ring-throwing game. John threw a ring, and it landed in the correct bottle. He exclaimed, "Hurray, Lisa... Look, it landed!" The shopkeeper asked who he had been speaking to.

When John showed Lisa, she wasn't there. When John looked around, he saw her standing near the giant wheel. He then gave the gift to her—a big yellow teddy bear. It was so cute that she became very happy. They then got on the giant wheel. As they ascended and the light transitioned from darkness to brightness, John could see Lisa's face clearly. He noticed her eyes. Those eyes, that face, reminded him of someone he knew well. There were similarities that struck him deeply.

The giant wheel continued to turn. Lisa slowly moved closer and sat beside John. She held his hand and looked into his eyes.

I know you're facing some challenges that are troubling you. You don't have to share those things with me if you're not ready. But if you want to talk about them, I'm here to listen. I want to tell you something that has been in my heart since I met you. Your presence brings me so much happiness. I feel safe when you're around. I don't want to lose you. When you didn't meet me for a week, I felt like I was dying over and over again. That's when I realized how special you are to me. I promise to always make you happy. I can't imagine my life without you. I LOVE YOU, John. Will you hold my hand forever?

John felt like he had been struck by lightning. He pulled away from her hand abruptly. The giant wheel stopped instantly. He hurriedly got off and ran back to his house. He was crying uncontrollably. Holding onto that picture, he wept deeply. John secluded himself in the confines of his room for several days thereafter.

Later, his college reopened, and John found another route to get there, deliberately avoiding the path where he might encounter Lisa. This went on for a few days as John attempted to steer clear of her.

One day, when John returned home and entered his room, he was shocked to find Lisa sitting on his bed. After the initial shock wore off, John asked softly, "Hey, why are you here?"

"I'm here because I wanted to see you. Why haven't you met me for the last few days? Are you angry with me?" Lisa replied.

"No, no," John said slowly, guiding her out of his house discreetly to ensure his mom didn't notice. Later, John walked to the park with Lisa.

They sat on the stone bench. After a long period of silence, Lisa asked, "John, why don't you tell me your full name? Please tell me."

"John Robert Kingston," he answered.

"So I can call you 'Rob'?" Lisa suggested. John froze for a moment. His eyes ceased blinking, filled with tears as memories rushed through his mind like pages from a book. Lisa became nervous. "John, what's wrong? Did I say something wrong?"

John explained that he wanted to share a story with her. He began to tell his tale.

When I was a child, I used to visit my aunt's house where my cousin Clair lived. There was also a girl who was her neighbor—a cute girl with curly red hair that always hung over her forehead. She always wore a black frock. Her name was Isabel. The three of us were playmates, but Isabel and I often ended up in fights during our games. Despite that, whenever I visited, she would always join us. My parents adored her as if she were their own daughter. Isabel was incredibly smart and beautiful. Our families would visit each other frequently; we were like one extended family.

Gradually, we became adults, and Clair's marriage came. For the wedding, Isabel joined me for shopping. She was a lively girl. I don't know how she managed to bargain for things so wisely. I enjoyed those times that I spent with her. Clair's wedding was a blast. We were together all the time.

After many days, I went to Auntie's home. Isabel kept me company. We chilled at night, watching movies, telling horror stories, and so on. She sat really close to me, and I thought I would never get another chance. It was the right time. I quietly said in her ear, "I LOVE YOU." She was shocked and left without saying a word. I felt a little ashamed. When I got home, I called her, but she didn't pick up the phone. I texted her many times, but there were no replies. I became so desperate.

One day, my friends and I went to her house to meet her, but they weren't there. I found out they had gone somewhere. The next day was Saturday. Normally, I wouldn't play football at night if I had already played in the morning. However, that day, I decided to play at night. Initially, I thought I would take my mobile with me, but then I decided against it. Even though it was 50% charged, I left it to charge so I could use it later. When I returned home very late, I saw 7 missed calls on my phone. They were from Isabel, but I was stubborn and thought she would call again. Exhausted, I didn't turn on my internet and fell asleep.

The next day, Dad woke me up and urged me to get ready quickly. We had to go to Auntie's house immediately. I was eager to see Isabel. I got ready in 5 minutes. When we arrived, there was a crowd gathered outside Isabel's house. I knew she had elderly grandparents. Normally, I wouldn't enter a house where someone had passed away, but I wanted to be there for her. Inside, her grandparents were sitting on the sofa, crying. When I saw the person who had passed away, I was shocked and stunned. It was Isabel. Not a single tear fell from my eyes. I felt numb, like I was frozen in place.

They took her from there.

Everybody left. Dad took me to my aunt's home, and I sat with my cousin. When she saw me, she shouted, "Why didn't you pick up her call?"

Clair told me that Isabel was a cancer patient. They weren't here the last few days because they went for a check-up. The doctor said she had shown improvement, which made her very happy. She was sick, which is why she didn't respond when you proposed to her. She doesn't know how much longer she has to live. She didn't want you to be sad. She has loved you deeply since childhood, but she never told you. When she found out she was getting better, she wanted to tell you that she loved you too. That's why she called you so many times. At the very least, you could have responded to her messages. If you had, she might still be alive. She died because of you. You are responsible for her death. These words echo in my ears and break my heart. I sat motionless. I couldn't even move a finger. I was shattered.

When I got home, I checked my phone. She had texted me, "I LOVE YOU, ROB." I completely lost control. All my sorrow poured out at once. Tears filled my eyes, soaking my bed. I threw my phone and smashed it. I began destroying my room in a fit of rage. I was overwhelmed with guilt for what I had done. I believed Isabel died because of me; my ego killed her. My mental health deteriorated completely. My parents took me to numerous doctors and psychologists, but no one could help me; no one had a solution for my depression. Despite trying various exercises and yoga, I only began to feel slightly better. I couldn't bear staying in that house any longer, so my parents brought me here. After that, I didn't speak to anyone. I couldn't love anyone. But when I saw you, your eyes reminded me of hers. That's why I decided to befriend you. She was the only one who called me Rob. She passed away on February 7th, which was her birthday. She loved me more than anyone else. I caused her death on her birthday. That regret still haunts me, and I can't forgive myself.

Upon hearing all this, Lisa's eyes filled with tears, and she deeply regretted that she hadn't known about this before. She apologized to John and offered him her hand. "Friends?" she asked. John smiled faintly and took her hand. They left the park together.

That night, John had a dream. In the dream, Lisa was sitting on a stone bench, and John approached her, touching her shoulder. When she turned to face him, John froze in place—it was Isabel. She was crying and asked John, "Why did you kill me?" Suddenly, John woke up from his sleep, realizing it was just a dream. However, Isabel's sorrowful face lingered in his heart.

The next day, John told Lisa about the dream. His regret was evident on his face. Lisa comforted him, saying, "Isabel must be happy for you. She wouldn't want to see you sad. It was just a dream. Let it go. I'm here for you as a friend, always. Don't worry, John." This reassurance made him so happy that he felt his heart begin to beat again.

Lisa walked with John to his house. She continued to console him, telling him not to dwell on the dream. They chatted at the gate before Lisa left. From inside the house, John's mother watched it. When John came inside, his mom asked who he had been talking to. John replied, "Oh, that's my friend Lisa." His mother seemed puzzled and said, "Your friend? I didn't see anyone there. I thought you were talking to yourself."

No, I was talking to my friend Lisa," John insisted as he went to his room. His mom, concerned, informed Dad about the situation. Dad approached John and asked, "What is your mom saying? Are you struggling with any addictions or something? Why do you talk to yourself?"

"Dad, why can't you understand? It was my friend Lisa, the only friend I have!" John shouted in frustration.

His mom decided to check the CCTV footage to confirm. She showed John the footage, revealing that there was nobody there when he was supposedly talking to Lisa. She also reviewed footage from previous days, where John appeared to be walking as if holding someone's hand. Overwhelmed with emotion, his mom began to cry.

John, what happened to you, my dear son?

"Why are you like this? Are you alright?" John was also feeling confused. He didn't understand what was happening to him. Was it all his imagination? Was Lisa real? Was this happening because he was constantly thinking about Isabel? He couldn't find any answers.

Over the next few days, John didn't encounter Lisa anywhere. He grew increasingly desperate. Even though she might not have been real, she had been a good friend who tried to bring him happiness. John cherished the time he had spent with her.

Once, I loved a girl.

Once, I loved a ghost.

I don't know who she was.

I don't know what she was.

I just loved her with all my heart.

I just want her with me forever.

I believed she was the one for me.

I believed I was the one for her.

I saw home in her eyes.

I found love in her smile.

I was born when she loved me.

And I died when she left me.

I lived some days when she was with me.

One night, Lisa appeared in John's dream. John asked her, "Who are you? Are you real? I'm so confused. Is all of this happening because I keep remembering Isabel?"

Lisa replied, "Yes, John, I am real, but I am not alive. I was going to tell you eventually."

John was shocked. "Are you a ghost?"

"Yes," Lisa confirmed. "I died in a car accident. My real name is Isabel. My husband is John Kingston—John Ethan Kingston."

"What? A Kingston member? But I've never heard of him. How is this possible?" John was utterly bewildered.

Lisa continued, "I died on February 7th, 2019."

"What?" John was stunned once again. "But we met two months ago, and today is February 5th, 2019. How could you have died on February 7th?"

Suddenly, the dream abruptly ended.

The next day, John waited a lot for her. At last, she came to his room. He asked about last day's dream: Was that all real? She agreed that those were true. He asked her more about the things that she said in the dream. She began to say, John Ethan Kingston is a well-known scientist in England, like his father. He's famous, but not yet. He will be in 10 years. His father discovered so many things. All of them were mainly based on other universes. His father discovered so many other universes. By using that, Ethan not only found but also created so many universes. And there is a valid reason for that. John asked, What was that?

She continued, "This world isn't like what you think. There is not only one John Kingston. In the universes that Ethan created, there are all one John Kingston and Isabel. But their middle name is different. Every one of the Kingstons fell in love with Isabel. But none of them got her. The thing that surprised me is that in this universe, there are two John Kingstons. John Ethan Kingston is also living in this universe. He is living in England now. This surprised me—two John Kingstons in the same world."

You once told me that you always have a feeling like déjà vu or something. Yeah, that's true; it's happening because whatever you are doing while experiencing déjà vu, a parallel version of you is doing it in a different universe simultaneously, thereby creating an alignment between the two universes. That's the reason for it.

"It all happened because of me," John asked. "What have you done?"

"It was on my birthday. He was so late. So I called Ethan, but it wasn't actually John shouting at me. When I called him that day, he suddenly yelled at me. Maybe it was because of work pressure."

I was afraid and tense. I took the car myself, even though I don't really know how to drive. John had warned me several times not to drive alone due to my anxiety. But that day, I drove to him. Halfway there, a boy jumped in front of my car. I swerved, hitting a tree. I lost consciousness. When I woke up, I was in another place. I ran home, where John was, but he couldn't hear me. Suddenly, I heard a voice from behind: "ETHAN." When I turned, I saw myself walking toward me, passing without touching. It was then I realized I was dead. Checking the date, it was 2018. I left and ran away, feeling Ethan's presence somewhere. I followed it and discovered that Ethan had created numerous universes in 2029, unintentionally disrupting the entire timeline. I believe that incident created me, and unfortunately, I ended up in 2018.

I wandered through every universe, but nobody could see me. You are the only one who saw me. Once, I found John Alfred Kingston. Even though he couldn't see me, he could recognize my presence. When he first saw my shadow in a room, he fell unconscious. John Alfred Kingston and his love, Isabel, were trapped in a dream world. Just before it collapsed, he heard my voice.

Then I found myself in a universe, which I consider the worst of them all. People there were afflicted by a virus called Zormus. Similar to zombies, John Mikeal Kingston lived there. He died because of me. His Isabel was alone in her house, and he was going to bring her to his house. Unfortunately, his niece Lily saw me and cried. I don’t know how she saw me. All the Zorms came for him, and... I still have that in mind. I can't forget that incident.

Those two worlds were also created by Ethan. Evidence in the factory showed that all this research was done by Ethan. He did it because he wanted me to return to his world, and he wanted to live with me. His greatest wish was to live with me forever. He loves me so much. I realized all these things from there. Ethan became very desperate after my death. He had never touched alcohol before, but my departure made him turn to drink. He did everything for me.

John said that if he were in Ethan's place, he would also do the same. He always wished to do something for his Isabel, but he couldn't. So, John decided to help her. He asked, "It's February 5th, and there are 2 days left. Tell me everything about that accident so we can stop it. Where did it happen? How did it happen? Then I can help you."

It's just February 5th; Isabel is still alive; maybe I can save her. But Lisa refused, "If you do that, then you will lose your existence." John insisted, "It's not a problem. It should happen. Maybe it will make you live again. That guy loves you so much, so I got a chance to save you. If I don't do so, that will be the greatest cruelty to him. He wants his Isabel back." But she was not ready. She said that he would lose his existence. Despite this, John decided to save her and all the other John Kingstons who were suffering. He hated his life. There was no mean to live this life.

John asked her about the incident. She slowly started, "It was about 7 o'clock in the evening. I was driving to him. When I reached the halfway point, a boy jumped in front of my car. I swerved suddenly, and it struck a tree. I had started from home exactly at 7:00." She told him the exact route they had to travel—it was 1000 kilometers to reach there.

They started their journey that day itself. The day was February 7th. Halfway through, his car developed a problem. They were almost there. He checked the time; it was almost 7 p.m., and he knew he couldn't make it to her house. So, he left the car there and ran towards her place. He ran quickly. He saw her car and rushed towards it. Unfortunately, John fell in front of Isabel's car. Isabel swerved, and it struck a tree. The accident happened suddenly, without any warning. When John stood up, he slowly approached the vehicle's door. He could see that Isabel was dead. He became scared and ran away. After a long run, he sat on a stone. Lisa came near him. Her sad face made John cry. "I'm so sorry; I couldn't save her, and I am the reason for everything." "It's not your fault. Everything happens because of me. I am destroying myself every time." All this will surely happen. It may be a cycle. Things are happening in a repetitive way. Ethan didn't just mess up the timeline; he created a cycle that repeats every time. We have nothing to do with that. She comforted him, but John fell into deep sadness and regret. He left the place and went to his house. Lisa also accompanied him. Those were sleepless nights. At a midnight, Lisa came to him and informed him that she was leaving. There is no purpose if she stays. John was disappointed. He opened his heart and begged. "Can't you stay for me as my Isabel? When I am with you, I can feel all the happiness, and I forget everything when you are around me. Won't you be there forever with me?" Tears of joy were coming from her eyes. She agreed to stay there.

Those were their days of love, laughter, and happiness. It became usual for Lisa to accompany him to college. Being invisible, she helped them expose those friends who bullied John by knowing their secrets through Lisa. John enjoyed it one day during an exam. Lisa came and helped him answer the questions. He realized he could use her for his success. John informed her about this and said, "Let's do it together." As she loved John very much, she agreed.

Once, they participated in a quiz competition at the international level, with a $1 million cash prize as the reward. In the first round, Lisa helped him from college so he could answer every question, and he won that round.

The final round took place in Australia. The initial questions were very simple, but John couldn't answer them because Lisa was not there. Suddenly, she appeared, and John answered the rest of the questions like a genius. He won the competition and the $1 million prize.

Eventually, John became lazy and greedy. With Lisa's help, he cracked all the competitive exams and gradually became a successful businessman. However, his character began to change. He became entirely greedy, cheating everyone to gain wealth, even forgetting the secret behind his success. His growth peaked, and he became a popular celebrity worldwide, earning vast amounts at a young age. He became powerful and rich, buying numerous cars of his own. He dropped his last name, Kingston, so the other John in the world couldn't recognize him. 'John Robert Kingston' became 'John Robert', a ruler who built his own kingdom through deceit. Before long, John spent nights with Lisa, filled with joy for both of them. However, now he is busy with work, solely focused on money. He no longer has time for Lisa. When she approached him, he only talked about his business and directed her to deceive the next person.

The next day onward, Lisa was missing. John just doesn't really care about that. But the other day, John had an important meeting. He really needs the help of Lisa, but she didn't come. John was frustrated. He failed to complete that meeting. Even though he memorized her a lot, she didn't even come.

On that night, John had a dream; Lisa was sitting on a stone bench, her face covered. When John went near her and touched her shoulder, she was sobbing pathetically. John was helpless. He asked what had happened. Lisa slowly answered, "I was not really dead in that car accident; actually, I am dead now." John suddenly came out of his dream. He was fully sweating. He came to reality and deeply thought about what he had done. He himself was ashamed of his worthless character. And he became very disappointed of his character towards Lisa. He realized that he even forgot about his love while running after money. Again, he fell into a deep depression. His mind was full of regrets, and he didn't care about his business anymore. He left all of his wealth and money behind. He sold all his cars except one. Now, he had nothing in his hand but his life.

My heart is broken.

Broken by love

My heart is aching.

Aching by love

Now I have a completed heart.

A heart that is not broken is an incomplete heart.

A heart becomes complete only when it is broken by love.

My heart is complete.

But it is broken.

Aching with memories

My heart is crying.

Even if my eyes don't

Now I have a completed, broken heart.

A few years passed like this. Every year, on Lisa's birthday, he missed her dearly. When they were together, they always celebrated her birthday with joy. Another February 7th arrived: Lisa's birthday. John thought she wouldn't come back to him, but he could reach out to her. He wrote a letter to her:

Hey Lisa…

I've been searching for you everywhere, but I can't find you. Where are you now? You took my heart with you when you suddenly disappeared, but you forgot to take yours back. Another year has gone by without you, and today is your birthday. I wish you were here. I can't live without you. I will always look for you, even if it's in hell, and I believe I'll see you wandering in heaven with angels. If you can see me from there, just give me that 1000-watt smile of yours, so I can feel alive again. I know I'm the one who has done wrong, always, and I don't want to live with that anymore. Every year, I've promised myself you'd come back, but you haven't. Love is a promise we make to our own hearts. I know all John Kingstons have the same faith as me. I'm trying to free myself from this agony because I'm the person who killed two people who loved me most, and I can't bear that regret; it's eating me alive. My heart died when you left me, Lisa, and I hope no one ever has to experience this kind of faithfulness. I fear I'm the worst John Kingston among all John Kingstons. Our story never had a beginning, so there will be no ending. I love you, Lisa.

He took his red and black Porsche car, which had been Lisa's favorite. He decided to die the same way she had died. He drove the car at excessive speed, and it collided with a tree.

John opened his eyes, and a doctor came to him.

Doctor: Hey…Welcome back Ryan

Incomplete love stories made love so much beautiful

PART 5

NOT ABOUT THE DREAM

THE REAL STORY

THE ONE WHO WAITS IS THE ONE WHO SUFFERS MORE

TIME 6:31

Ryan woke up after hearing his mother's voice.

Hey Richie, wake up; it's time to go to school." Ryan Richard was starting 9th grade. It was his first day of the school year, and he was happier than ever because the girl he had loved since 7th grade had joined his school. He went to school early that day, eagerly waiting for her. When she arrived, he introduced her to his friends, saying, "She's the one I've always talked about. Her name is Freya. I've loved her so much for almost 3 years." As she passed by, she smiled at him—a 1000-watt smile. She already knew that Ryan had feelings for her.

Days passed, and Ryan made many friends in her class. He confided in them about his feelings, and they all started to help him.

In December, he attended a 3-day camp and made two best friends from Freya's class, Dana and Jiya. They informed him that Freya knows about him and they believe she feels the same way. This news made him incredibly happy. From the camp, he didn't just gain two best friends; he gained two sisters who meant the world to him. They supported him in everything.

During an arts day event, he decided to confess his feelings to Freya. His friends let her know that Ryan wanted to talk to her. When she approached him, Ryan once again found himself captivated by her beauty. She had big, beautiful, deep brown eyes that shimmered like honey in sunlight, framed by long lashes that brushed her cheeks when she smiled. Her lips were pale pink, pouty, and full like rosebuds. Her almond-colored skin complemented her deep brown hair perfectly, and she wore a white dress for her group song performance at the arts festival, looking like an angel.

She asked him why he had called her over. Overwhelmed by her beauty, he couldn't find the words to speak. She then asked how her dress looked, to which he replied, "You look like a princess, Freya." She responded with a knowing smile that enchanted him. Her smile was what had originally captured his heart.

He always wanted to see her happy. She invited him to watch her performance and returned to her team. However, Ryan couldn't move from where he stood, unable to forget the image of her smiling in that white dress. Her smile had planted a flower in his heart. He fell for her eyes once more and was prepared to fall for her a million times over. Every day, he longed to see her smile and to fall in love with her repeatedly. No matter how much time passed, he only wished for her happiness because he cared for her more than himself. He loved her more than anything.

Oh, I want to hug you for once.
Once is enough.
I just want to know how it feels.
And I just want to feel it.
Feel it's every moment
I want to feel your heart.
And it's beatings.
I want to feel your happiness.
And sadness
I can fix your heart.
And I can make you smile again.
You stole my heart.
You stole my soul.
Keep it
Just keep it.

He went to her program, and afterward, he approached her again. She asked him about her performance. He replied, "Oh, sorry, I didn't see it. I forgot." "I saw you in the crowd. Don't lie to me, Richie," they both laughed. He told her, "You already knew why I called you, and I wanted to know your opinion about that." "Oh, is that it? I don't want to be in a relationship right now, I'm afraid of my parents, and we're also neighbors. I hope you understand, Ryan," she told him before leaving. He felt deeply saddened and shared this with his friends. They tried to comfort him.

One day later, it was sports day. He won prizes for running races, which made him proud because Freya was there to see his victories. That day, he decided he would become the sports champion of the school next year to make her proud. He started working hard in sports and football. He got selected for a big club, which made him happy, and he became popular in school, attending many matches. Afterward, he was selected for a district club. All of this made him happy because he did it all to make her proud.

One day, while playing for his district club, he was staring at her picture on his phone. One of his teammates noticed and asked Ryan about her. He happily shared everything: they had been friends for a long time, played together as kids, and watched horror movies together. "When she enjoyed the movie, I enjoyed watching her," he said. "Now I'm here because of her." His teammate asked how. "It's for her; I worked hard to make her proud. I've put in so much effort for this, and one day I will make her mine," said Ryan.

His friend asked, "Ryan, tell me one moment that you will never forget that you had with her." Ryan described it with a smile on his face: "It was a rainy day; I was traveling on a bus. I got the window seat, and I was enjoying the cold wind. At that moment, I had a positive feeling, so I looked around. I saw Freya sitting next to my seat. She didn't see me; she was sleeping. So I just sat beside her. I didn't wake her up; I just sat there and admired her beauty. She didn't notice me. I left before she woke up. It was the one moment I will never forget, and I will always remember that day. God gave me a chance to admire her beauty so closely. That was the best moment."

Ryan returned to school after the tournament, and the whole school appreciated his achievement. Then the annual day arrived. He had been watching her for a long time. She eventually approached him and explained, "It's not because I don't love you; it's because I am afraid of my parents." This statement left him feeling both happy and sad.

Later that night, she texted him, asking, "Did my words hurt you today?" He replied, "No, I can understand." Her text brought him immense happiness, and he read it almost a thousand times. That year became the best year of his life; nothing was the same afterward. It marked the beginning of Ryan Richard's downfall. He lost everything he had achieved after that year.

Days passed, and he felt like he was growing distant from her, so he confided in Dana. She suggested an idea. They both played a game where Dana instructed him to approach one of Freya's friends and tell her that he had stopped loving Freya. Ryan followed Dana's advice precisely, and it worked. Freya became upset and asked Ryan about the problem, but he didn't respond to her; he avoided her all day.

On that night, she texted him and asked, "What's the matter?" He decided not to reply to her and sent some random letters instead, planning to delete the message so it would show as deleted for everyone.

However, he accidentally clicked "delete for me" instead. Because of this mistake, he decided to respond to her message. He replied that there was no problem at all. Unfortunately, this message was read by her mother, who confronted her and made her reveal everything.

Ryan was attending his cousin's wedding at the time and was unaware of these events. When he returned, his best friend informed him about what had transpired, putting him in a difficult situation. He never forgets that date: February 7th, 2019. He cried a lot. Afterward, Freya became very afraid and avoided him completely. This deeply affected Ryan, leaving him unsure of what to do. He sought advice from everyone, but no one had a solution.

The following year at school, her class became closer to his, and she eventually started looking at him again, which gave him some relief. She told her friends that she would never love Ryan and couldn't love him, and they relayed this to him. He decided not to disturb her further, but he couldn't stop loving her; his feelings never waned.

Then sports day arrived, and as he had promised himself, he became the sports champion. When he received the trophy, one of his friends handed it to Freya, who congratulated him. This made him incredibly happy, and that night, he slept peacefully for the first time in a long while.

At the annual day of that year, he asked her once more if there was any hope for them. Unfortunately, there was none. So, he suggested they remain friends.

He felt as though he had lost everything. Years passed, things changed, but his love for her remained steadfast.

One day, Jiya told him something she had kept from Ryan. She revealed that Freya also loved him deeply, and Freya had confided in her, saying, "It's because my mother caught Ryan's message; otherwise, we would be in a relationship now." These words felt like rocks falling on Ryan's chest. That day changed everything for him. He felt like he had lost his world. He deeply regretted his actions and couldn't forget what had happened. He fell into utter depression and couldn't forgive himself. His carelessness had ruined everything. This revelation made him believe he was one step closer to winning her heart, and she was almost his.

You were one step closer to me.

And I lost you.

You were almost mine.

And that almost still hurts me.

You wrote your name in my heart.

And left me without erasing it.

I wish I could re-live that day.

That day, I lost you forever.

I wish I never saw you because

That hurts me more than I thought.

I can see you with my eyes closed.

I can feel you in my every breath.

My body heals all wounds very quickly.

I don't know why my heart can't heal anything.

When you planted a flower in my heart with your eyes,

I thought you would water it every day with your smile.

The day I lost you

The day I lost myself

Because of that, several times he tried hard again to express his love, but unfortunately, those were futile attempts. Initially, she wasn't convinced at all. She rejected him. He passed 10th and 11th grades, but in his mind, she remained the same.

When he was in 12th grade, she joined the same school again. His feelings for her increased once more, and his love reached its peak. After finishing 12th grade, she became such an addiction to him that he couldn't give up. Many of his friends advised him to move on and choose a different path for his life, trying to convince him that it would be better for him. But he was never ready to leave her. He couldn't imagine loving anyone else; he loved her with all his heart.

Ryan's cousins and friends scolded him and urged him to let her go. But he couldn't; every night he cried thinking about her. He became an introvert. He didn't know what to do. One day his best friend told him that he would forget her once he committed to someone else. "I know it's so hard for you, but you'll be okay when someone else comes into your life," his friend said. However, Ryan refused to consider that. His friend pleaded with him to move on, saying, "I can't see you like this anymore; you have to move on."

After a difficult period, Ryan decided to move on. He proposed to other girls, and while some accepted and others rejected, he couldn't follow through. He explained he wasn't ready for a relationship and avoided further proposals. He realized he couldn't love anyone other than Freya.

These were still stressful days for him. He didn't turn to drugs but instead went to the gym and played football, though nothing eased his pain. Years passed, but his heart remained full of regrets. The situation with Freya continued to weigh heavily on him. Sometimes Freya would mention that the issue was their proximity; otherwise, things might have been different. Every setback broke him, but he refused to give up on her. Throughout his life, he had only loved one girl, and because of that, his life felt ruined, though his love for her never faltered.

To cope, he began writing whatever came to mind. Only a pained heart could produce such poignant words. He wrote poems and quotes about his love for Freya, his pain, and everything in between. Eventually, the idea of writing a book emerged. He had been contemplating a theme for years and started penning his life experiences, weaving in his love for Freya. He created characters resembling them and titled the book "I WAS NEVER THE ONE," feeling he had never been the right person for her.

Upon publication, the book gained popularity, yet his ultimate goal remained unfulfilled—Freya had not read it, leaving him desperate.

One day, Freya decided to read the book. The experience deeply moved her; tears streamed down her face as she realized how much Ryan loved her and the effort he had poured into his life. She concluded that no one else could be as worthy of her as him and decided to call him. Studying far from home, she reached out to Ryan, who was overjoyed and speechless at her call.

He went there. They both went to a park and sat on a stone bench. She looked into his eyes and asked, "Do you have anything to say?" Tears were shedding from his eyes. This was the moment that he had expected for the last 8 years. He began to say each and everything. She was so surprised. She hugged him. "How can you love me so much? You have sacrificed so much for me for the last 8 years. Am I that special?" In my eyes, you are more special than everything. I didn't fall in love with you because I needed you, because I wanted someone to hold me, or because I needed you to make me feel loved. I fell in love with you because the moment I met you, everything stopped. The sounds around us were all muted, and all I could hear was your voice. Every time I stared into your eyes, I felt at home, and I had no other thought in the world. But how do I make you happy for the rest of your life because you already do so much for me and you didn't even know it? But as time went on, you slowly started to drift away, and the worst part of it was that I knew I couldn't do anything to stop it from happening. You were gone, but you always have a place in my heart, whether I like it or not, because I have never felt for anyone like that.

I thought I had gamophobia or something, but now I know it's because of you, and it's always you that stopped me from everything. My friend once told me that "incomplete love stories made love so beautiful," but I believed that one day you would be mine, and at this moment I'm also living with that hope. Is there any chance for that?

"I also loved you, but I was afraid to express it. Now, anything could happen, but I love you. I want to live the rest of my life with you." Ryan felt like a dream. He jumped because of happiness. He felt like the entire world was his. He lifted Freya up and ran. They shared their love. Then he returned.

Like God is playing games with them, when he got his love, an unfortunate thing happened. He met with an accident on the way. He was in a coma for 10 years. When he opened his eyes, he saw everyone running.

A doctor came to him and said, "Hey, welcome back, Ryan Richard." He was surprised when he told him that his name is not Ryan Richard; his name is John Kingston. He asked about Isabel: "Where is Isabel? I want to see her. I want to see her now." The doctor understood his problem, and the doctor asked him, "Do you remember anything?" He told the doctor the full story of him and Isabel.

After that, the doctor asked the nurse to bring something. It was a book. The book is written by Ryan Richard himself. "I WAS NEVER THE ONE." The doctor said, you told the stories that you wrote in your book. That's not the real story. Then the doctor and his parents explained to him the real story. After some time, he realized the truth. He wanted to see Freya. He asked the doctor, what's the date today, and the doctor said it's February 7th, 2034. He asked God, why he always plays with me. What have I done to do this to me? He cried a lot.

When he came out of the hospital, he searched for Freya everywhere, but he couldn't find her. There was no one in their house. He asked everybody about them, but nobody told him anything. After one year, he finally found her house. He was so excited to see her after years. He had a doubt about whether she got married, that would never happen. I know she is waiting for me.

He reached there. When he entered her house, her family was looking at him very rudely. He asked, where is Freya; is she married? Is she in-laws' house? Her brother hit him, threw him out of their house, and threw an 11-year-old newspaper. He was stoned when he went through the headline.

"Two friends met with an accident; the girl named Freya Isabel died at the spot, and the boy, Ryan Richard Kingston, was taken to the hospital with major injuries."

He forgot that she was with him.

Maybe in the next life I will make it right, till then bye.

He felt love

He was in love

He got his love

He lost his love.

I WAS NEVER THE ONE

Some love stories never end. Some love stories never start to end. People do anything for their love. Sometimes they are unbelievable. Some people are so lucky that they experienced love, and there are some people who are not lucky enough to know the beauty of love because they all loved the wrong person at the wrong time. It's not about fiction or fantasy; it's about love. Undying love that a man had for a woman. Everyone has their own time. Just wait for the right moment, and your love will find you in a wind that God made only for you. All you have to do is wait, wait for the moment, and wait for the wind. If you are ready to wait, then you also need to be ready for suffering. The one who waits is the one who suffers more. If you have the power to love someone for so long, then God will make sure that your love finds its way. All you have to do is hang in there and wait. Wait for your time.

MUHAMMED ANSHID

AUTHOR'S NOTE

Thank you for reading my book. This is my first ever book. I know there are a lot of mistakes in it because I wrote it without reading any other books. One day I saw my brother reading a book and thought, why can't I read a book? That's when my inner self asked me, why are you reading other people's books when you can write your own book? Ha-ha! So I decided to write my own book. I challenged myself that the first book I ever read would be written by me. Now, after 3 years of hard work, I have finally completed my book. Thank you, brother; unknowingly, you are the reason for all of this. Thanks to all who supported me on this journey.

ABOUT THE BOOK

This book revolves around five different stories with the same main characters, all centered on the theme of love and dreams. In all five stories, the protagonist faces challenges in finding love, and he's dreaming about his favorite person. It's a sci-fi love story. Throughout the story, the character is trying harder and making sacrifices for his love. He considers her his whole world. All this happens because of love. The main character, John Kingston, does everything he can to win back his love.

AUTHOR PROFILE

Muhammed Anshid M is a talented individual born in the beautiful region of Wayanad, Kerala, in 2004. He is a passionate football player who enjoys the thrill of the game both on and off the field. With a supportive family and a love for sports, Muhammed Anshid M is on a path to success both academically and athletically. By introducing his first book, he has now entered the world of writing.